OBI,
Gerbil ON A School Trip!

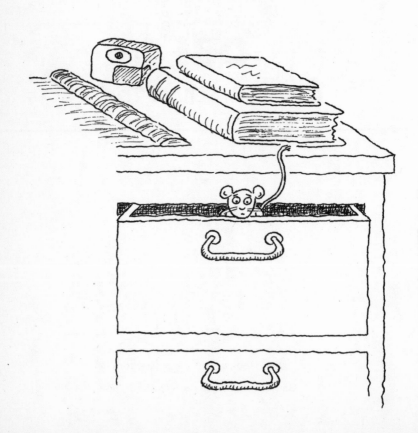

OBI,
Gerbil ON A School Trip!

M. C. Delaney

Dial Books for Young Readers

An imprint of Penguin Group (USA) Inc.

DIAL BOOKS FOR YOUNG READERS

A division of Penguin Young Readers Group • Published by the Penguin Group

Penguin Group (USA) Inc., 375 Hudson Street, New York, New York 10014, USA

USA | Canada | UK | Ireland | Australia | New Zealand | India | South Africa | China

Penguin Books Ltd, Registered Offices: 80 Strand, London WC2R 0RL, England

For more information about the Penguin Group visit penguin.com

Library of Congress Cataloging-in-Publication Data

Delaney, M. C. (Michael Clark)

Obi, gerbil on a school trip!/by M.C. Delaney.

p. cm.

Summary: While trying to find out who Rachel chose as her favorite pet,
Obi the gerbil gets trapped in Rachel's backpack and winds up at school, where
she learns new things and makes some friends.

ISBN 978-0-8037-3854-6

[1. Schools—Fiction. 2. Gerbils—Fiction. 3. Pets—Fiction.
4. Friendship—Fiction.] I. Title.

PZ7.D37319Oam 2013 [Fic]—dc23 2012039101

Printed in the United States of America

1 3 5 7 9 10 8 6 4 2

Designed by Jason Henry • Text set in Century Schoolbook

The publisher does not have any control over and does not assume
any responsibility for author or third-party websites
or their content.

To Lucia Monfried,
who helped bring Obi
into this world

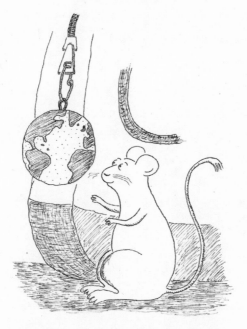

And for all the school librarians,
teachers, and children, who helped
keep her in it

Contents

OBI,
Gerbil on a School Trip!

Prologue

It didn't happen
often, but sometimes Obi
couldn't help but feel, well, just a little insecure
about things.

It's easy to see why. For starters, she was a female
gerbil with a boy's name. In all honesty, Obi really
didn't mind having a boy's name—after all, many
Human girls these days have names that used to be
thought of as boys' names.

But in Obi's case, the reason *she* had a boy's name
was because Rachel Armstrong, Obi's ten-year-old
adoptive mother, thought she was a *boy* gerbil! In
fact, *all* the Armstrongs thought Obi was a boy gerbil! That was because Obi was only a few days old
when Rachel and her father had stopped into a pet
store to buy Obi. At that point in Obi's young life,

nobody could tell if she was a boy or a girl, not even the woman in the pet store. Which was why Rachel had named her new pet gerbil after her favorite character in *Star Wars*—the great Jedi knight (and man), Obi-Wan Kenobi. All this time later, everyone *still* thought Obi was a male gerbil—nobody had thought to check to see if, just perhaps, they might be mistaken.

To add to her insecurity, Obi, who had once been Rachel's only pet, now had to share Rachel with not one but two—yes, *two*—other pets: a golden retriever puppy named Kenobi and a little gerbil named Wan!

Notice anything *odd* about those two names? Yes, that's right, they have Obi's name! Rachel gave Kenobi and Wan *her* name—or parts of her name, at any rate! So not only did Obi now have to share her adoptive mother with Kenobi and Wan, she had to share *her* name with them as well!

At least there was one thing Obi did not have to worry about, though. She had the satisfaction of knowing she was Rachel's favorite pet. This gave Obi incredible peace of mind, put a little bounce in her step, gave her an easy heart. She knew that, of the three of them, it was she, not Kenobi or Wan, whom Rachel loved most. It was she, not Kenobi or Wan, whom Rachel would want to be stuck with on a desert island. Not that Rachel—or Obi, for that matter—wanted to be stuck on a desert island!

You agree, don't you? That Obi was Rachel's favorite pet?

Silly question, right? Yes, of course, you agree! How could Obi *not* be Rachel's favorite pet?

Uh, you know, you could look a bit more sure about this than you do! You really could!

Oh, my gosh! What if Obi was wrong!? What if she *wasn't* Rachel's favorite pet!? What if it was Kenobi or—horror of horrors—Wan!? What would Obi do? How would she deal with such a thing?

Well, there's only one way to find out—you'll just have to read the story! That's all there is to it!

But, hurry, will you—for Obi's sake!

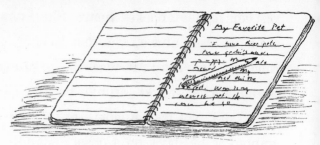

It was all Mr. Durkins's fault! It was all because of him that Wan was chewing on the bars of his cage again!

Wan was not chewing on his bars because his little gerbil teeth were coming in and he needed something to gnaw on. *That*, Obi felt, would be understandable! Annoying, yes, but understandable!

Nor was he doing it to get Rachel's attention. That, too, would be understandable. After all, Obi herself sometimes gnawed on the bars of her cage to get Rachel to glance over. As soon as she did, Obi would stop gnawing instantly.

No, Wan was chewing on the bars of his cage for no other reason than to get on Rachel's nerves!

Rachel was at her desk on the other side of the bedroom, trying to do her homework. Pencil in hand, a look of deep concentration on her face, Rachel leaned over her desk and wrote in her spiral-bound notebook. Wan, meanwhile, was in his cage, gnawing away, being as annoying as anything, trying desperately to shatter that look of deep concentration on Rachel's face.

It was all because of Mr. Durkins that Wan was being so annoying. Mr. Durkins was the old, bitter mouse who lived up in the Armstrongs' attic. He hated the Armstrongs! He loathed every single one of them, even—if you can believe it—Obi's dear, sweet adoptive mother! Apparently, Mr. Durkins had only one goal in life: to make the Armstrongs' lives absolutely miserable!

He was an evil mouse, Mr. Durkins! His new diabolical plan involved Wan. He had taught the little gerbil how to chew on the bars of his cage and had instructed Wan to do it as often as possible—but only when Rachel was in her bedroom. He knew the noise, grating as it was, would drive Rachel nuts.

And it did!

Wan, who didn't know any better, was only too happy to do whatever Mr. Durkins asked. Wan had become Mr. Durkins's little helper, his protégé. He did everything that nasty, little mouse told him to, no questions asked. Worse, Wan seemed to really enjoy doing as Mr. Durkins instructed. Right now, for instance, he was giggling to himself as he chewed on his bars. It made Wan sound so sinister! (Either that, or a gerbil with a serious giggling problem.)

Rachel was doing her best to ignore Wan. At one point, she cupped her hands over her ears so as not to hear him. But honestly, how can you write with your hands over your ears? You can't! Finally losing her temper, Rachel flashed a fierce look at Wan and snapped, "Will you stop it, Wan! You're driving me nuts! Can't you see I'm trying to do my homework?"

"Yes, Wan, knock it off, will you!" exclaimed Obi, squeaking in Gerbil. "You're driving *me* nuts, too!"

But did Wan listen to either Rachel or Obi? No! He kept right on gnawing—gnawing and giggling!

The thing was, Obi really wanted Rachel to do a good job on her homework. That afternoon Rachel had come home from school very excited. Tossing her backpack onto the floor of her bedroom, she fixed her eyes on Obi and said, "Guess what, Obi? Guess what my homework assignment for tonight is?"

Obi, who was in her cage, was startled. Since when did Rachel get so excited about homework? As far as Obi could tell, Rachel hated homework! Every evening, it seemed, she complained about how much homework she had to do. A school night didn't go by that Mrs. Armstrong didn't have to stick her head into Rachel's bedroom and ask her if she had done her homework yet. So what was so exciting about today's homework assignment? With a quizzical look on her small whiskered face, Obi peered at Rachel through the bars of her cage.

"I have to write a paper about my favorite pet! You'll never guess *who* that is!"

Obi smiled to herself. Oh, she had a pretty good idea! It was Obi, of course! Who else could it be? It certainly wasn't Wan, not with his incessant gnawing! And Obi was almost certain it wasn't Rachel's other pet, either, the golden retriever puppy, Kenobi. It might've been Kenobi once, back when he was a cute, little, helpless, and hapless puppy. But lately, Kenobi had been growing by leaps and bounds and no longer looked like the cuddliest thing on earth. The puppy was also no longer allowed to hang out up in Rachel's bedroom, the way he used to.

To be fair, this wasn't really Kenobi's fault. Mr. Armstrong had made it a rule that Kenobi, who was quite furry and tended to shed a lot, could no longer be upstairs where all the Armstrongs' bedrooms were located. But still! Had it been Obi, she would have found a way upstairs, rule or no rule! Nothing would ever keep *her* from being with Rachel! That was the kind of pet Obi was!

Obi's cage sat on top of Rachel's dresser, right beside Wan's cage. Obi went over to the side of her cage that faced Wan and glowered at the little gerbil. He was so busy chewing on the bars of his cage—and giggling to himself—he didn't even notice Obi.

"Stop gnawing, Wan!" Obi ordered.

Wan paid no attention.

"Did you hear me, Wan?"

Apparently not: he kept on gnawing and giggling!

"I SAID STOP GNAWING, WAN! STOP IT THIS INSTANT!"

That got Wan to stop! He turned and gave Obi a very bewildered look. "But Mr. D told me to chew on my bars when Rachel is in her bedroom."

Obi frowned. "Mr. D?"

"You know, Mr. Durkins! He told me to call him Mr. D!"

"He did?" Obi couldn't help but feel a little hurt. Mr. Durkins had never asked *her* to call him Mr. D. But then why would he? It wasn't like she and Mr. Durkins were friends. The fact was, Obi disapproved of everything Mr. Durkins did. "When did he ask you to do that?" she inquired.

"One time when you were asleep in your cage."

"Well, Wan," said Obi, "I really don't care what Mr. D—*Mr. Durkins*—told you to do! *I'm* telling you to *stop* gnawing!"

"But Mr. D won't like that!"

"I don't care! Rachel has a very important home-work assignment to do," explained Obi. "She needs you to be very quiet so she can concentrate. Your chewing on your bars is getting on Rachel's nerves!"

"But that's what Mr. D *wants* me to do!"

"Yes, I know but that's not what *I* want you to do!"

"But *you're* not Mr. D!"

Obi tried to stay calm. It wasn't easy! She wanted to wring Wan's little neck. Since that was out of the question, Obi did the next best thing: she glared at Wan. She gave him her most withering stare. Obi was trying to think of what else she could do (since her most withering stare didn't seem to be having much of an effect on Wan) when she heard Rachel chuckle to herself. Obi swung about and saw that Rachel had a smile on her face. The girl was at her desk, pencil in hand, smiling and staring straight ahead, completely lost in thought. Evidently, she had remembered some funny incident she had had with her favorite pet.

Obi smiled, too. She had no idea what happy memory Rachel had recalled, but it had to be something good. Was it that time she and

Rachel went to the gerbil convention together? They sure had a blast that day, didn't they?

All at once, Rachel began writing furiously again. For his part, Wan began gnawing furiously again. After a couple of minutes of intense writing, Rachel tossed her pencil down on the desk and blurted out, "Finished!"

Obi watched as Rachel ripped a sheet of paper out of her spiral-bound notebook. Leaping up from the desk, Rachel went over to her blue backpack, which was on the floor, unzipped it, and stuck in her homework paper.

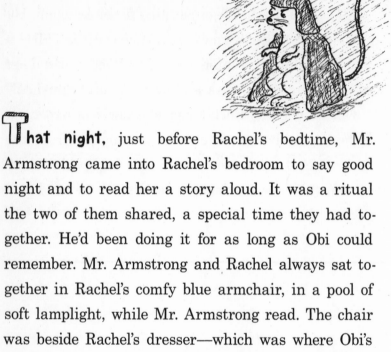

That night, just before Rachel's bedtime, Mr. Armstrong came into Rachel's bedroom to say good night and to read her a story aloud. It was a ritual the two of them shared, a special time they had together. He'd been doing it for as long as Obi could remember. Mr. Armstrong and Rachel always sat together in Rachel's comfy blue armchair, in a pool of soft lamplight, while Mr. Armstrong read. The chair was beside Rachel's dresser—which was where Obi's cage sat. Some evenings Mr. Armstrong read a book that could be finished in one sitting. Other times, he read a big book that took several evenings—sometimes even several weeks—to complete. Like tonight's book. They were reading *The Subtle Knife*, the second book in the trilogy His Dark Materials.

While Rachel, dressed in her jammies, cuddled up

close beside her father and listened, Obi sat in the bedroom tower of her cage, listening.

Yet, Obi wasn't *just* listening. As she listened, Obi was also peering down at the words on the pages of the book and connecting them to the words that Mr. Armstrong was reading aloud. It was by doing this that Obi, after many, many books, had learned how to read.

Yes, that's right, Obi could read! It was Obi's little secret—something no one else knew about. Well, except Mr. Durkins. He knew Obi could read. But that was only because he made it his business to know everybody else's business in the Armstrongs' house! Oh, and a couple of dogs in the neighborhood also knew Obi could read. (It's a long story, but Obi had told them she could read.) So maybe it wasn't such a big secret, after all.

Mr. Armstrong was at that part of the book in which Lyra and Will, the two main characters, had just entered another world. Will had used a knife, the subtle knife, to slice open a piece of air, which allowed Lyra and him to enter this new world. Obi, fascinated, was anxious to find out more about this other world.

But just then, Mrs. Armstrong came into the room to say good night to Rachel.

Mr. Armstrong stopped reading and said, "Well, I think this is where we'll stop for tonight." And with that, he marked the page with a piece of paper and closed the book! Obi was flabbergasted! How could Mr. Armstrong stop at such a suspenseful part of the story!?

"Oh, can't we read a little more?" begged Rachel.

Which was exactly what Obi was hoping Rachel would say! Obi and her adoptive mother were alike in so many ways. Rachel loved a good bedtime story just as much as Obi did.

"Sorry, kiddo, but it's beddy-bye time," said Mr. Armstrong. "You've got school tomorrow. Someone needs a good night's sleep."

Rachel, who slept on the top bunk of a bunk bed, climbed the ladder up to her bed and slipped under the covers. Mr. Armstrong tucked her in and gave her a good-night kiss on top of her head. As he left the room, he turned off the lights.

Now that the room was dark, Obi nestled down under a big pile of cedar shavings in her bedroom tower.

She closed her eyes to go to sleep. But she couldn't sleep. She was too wired. She couldn't stop thinking about the story Mr. Armstrong had read. She kept wondering about this new world that Lyra and Will had entered and what it would be like. It was driving Obi crazy not knowing!

The lights hadn't been off for more than a few minutes when Obi, still wide awake, heard a slow, deep, steady, rhythmic breathing sound coming from the upper bed of the bunk bed—it was the sound Rachel always made when she was asleep. Then Obi heard Wan rustling about in his cage. Then, just like that, the rustling stopped, which meant that Wan, too, had fallen asleep.

Obi tried again to go to sleep. It was no use, though. She was too excited. How Obi wished she could enter a new world.

Suddenly Obi's eyes flung open. She had the eerie sensation that someone was on the dresser outside her cage, lurking in the darkness! Her heart now pounding wildly, Obi peered down from her domed bedroom tower.

She let out a startled gasp. A small dark figure, a shadowy smudge, stood on the dresser between her cage and Wan's.

It was Darth Vadar!

No, wait, that wasn't Darth Vadar! Straining to see in the darkness, Obi now saw it was Mr. Durkins. He was standing up on his hind legs, all hunched over. In the inky darkness, he looked just like Darth Vadar!

Obi slipped down the tube that connected her bedroom tower and the lower level of her cage. "Mr. Durkins!" she said, speaking to him through the bars of her cage. "What are you doing here?"

"Oh, just looking in on Boy Wonder."

Obi frowned. "Boy Wonder? Who's that?" Then, all at once, she knew. "Oh, no! You're not talking about Wan, are you?"

"I sure am!" replied Mr. Durkins. "I'm so proud of my boy! He did a super-good job today!"

"First of all, Mr. Durkins, he's not your boy. And what do you mean he did a super-good job? Doing what?"

"Annoying Rachel, of course! Did you see the way he got her to lose her temper? The boy is a natural!"

Obi shook her head in disbelief and dismay. Mr. Durkins may not have been Darth Vadar, but he was just as evil!

Mr. Durkins turned and peered into Obi's cage. He fixed his eyes on Obi and said, "So who do you think she wrote about?"

"Excuse me?"

"Rachel. Who do you think she wrote about? You know, for her homework paper. Who do you think she said is her favorite pet?"

Obi, shocked, stared at Mr. Durkins's shadowy, hunched figure. As dark as the bedroom was, Obi was still able to make out the stern, hard look in his beady eyes.

"How did you know Rachel had to write a homework paper about her favorite pet?"

"Nothing happens in this house without me knowing about it, kid! So who do you think she wrote about? Think she wrote about you?"

"Me?" said Obi, trying to sound surprised. She gave a small, modest laugh. "Oh, heavens no, not me!"

"Yeah, you're right," said Mr. Durkins. "No way would she write about you."

"Wait, what!?" exclaimed Obi, taken aback. "What do you mean no way would she write about me? Rachel most certainly would so write about me! Why wouldn't she?"

"Why *would* she?" said Mr. Durkins. "You're her oldest pet!"

"I'm not *that* old!" protested Obi. "And besides, what does that have to do with anything?"

"Well, you've been around the longest."

"Yes, that's true, but I still don't see why that would stop her from writing about me."

"Well, I think it's perfectly obvious," said Mr. Durkins. "She's grown tired of you!"

"She has not!"

"You're sure about that, kid?"

"Yes, I'm sure! And don't call me kid! Rachel has not grown tired of me!"

"Okay, if you say so."

"I'm telling you she hasn't!" insisted Obi.

"Okay, she hasn't!" said Mr. Durkins.

"She really hasn't!"

"I said okay, okay?" replied Mr. Durkins.

"You may say okay, Mr. Durkins, but you don't mean okay!"

"Well, you *have* been her pet the longest. It's only natural for her to grow tir— what was *that*?"

"What was what?" asked Obi, glancing about.

"There it is again! Did you hear it?"

"Hear what?" asked Obi, who hadn't heard a thing.

"There was a little scuffle downstairs in the kitchen," said Mr. Durkins. "One of the cats just hissed at Junior."

By "Junior," Mr. Durkins meant the puppy, Kenobi. "Junior" was Mr. Durkins's less than flattering nick-name for the dog.

"Why would one of the cats do that?" asked Obi.

"Shh!" hushed Mr. Durkins.

Obi strained her ears to listen, but all she heard was Rachel breathing in her sleep.

"It's Sugar Smacks," said Mr. Durkins at last. "She caught Junior eating out of her cat food bowl again."

Obi stared at Mr. Durkins. "How do you know that?"

But then she answered her own question. "Never mind, I know. Nothing in this house escapes you!"

"I better go check this out!" said Mr. Durkins.

There were two ways to get down from Rachel's dresser. One way was to slide down the electrical cord of the lamp that was on the dresser. The other way was to do what Mr. Durkins did: he stepped over to the front edge of the dresser and just leaped off. For an old, crippled mouse, he certainly was spry! Obi watched as his small, dark form limped quickly across the bedroom carpet and disappeared into a tiny, dark smudge that was on the baseboard by the closet. It was the hole that led into the secret passageway.

Obi let out a heavy sigh. She hated talking with Mr. Durkins. She really did! It seemed like every time she talked with him, he said something that upset her. Obi had been so certain that she was Rachel's favorite pet and that Rachel had written about her. But now she wasn't so sure anymore! Could Mr. Durkins be right? Could Rachel have grown tired of Obi? Could Rachel have written about Kenobi or Wan instead? While Kenobi was no longer the irresistible, little, huggable puppy he once was, he had begun to learn some dog tricks. For instance, he could now lift his front paw whenever Rachel said, "Give me your paw!" And he could almost, but not quite, bring himself to surrender a tennis ball when Rachel threw it to him, expecting him to retrieve it.

And what about Wan? While he could be exasperating as all get out, he was pretty cute, being such a tiny gerbil. Tears filled Obi's eyes. Oh, why, why, why did Mr. Durkins, that horrible, disgusting, evil mouse, have to tell Obi that maybe Rachel had grown tired of her? Now Obi was having doubts—serious doubts!— that she was Rachel's favorite pet!

Feeling very sorry for herself, Obi let out another sigh. She knew there was only one way to find out.

She would just have to read Rachel's homework paper. Since Obi knew how to read, this would not be a problem. Nor was letting herself out of her cage and going into Rachel's backpack, where Rachel had put her homework paper.

In addition to being able to read, Obi had another secret. She knew how to slip in and out of her cage at will. So escaping from her cage wasn't a problem. No, the problem was that it was nighttime, and Obi needed light to be able to read. Which meant Obi needed to wait until morning when it would be light again. Could she wait that long? Well, it's not like she had much choice. Somehow, she would just have to! Turning, Obi climbed back up her tube to wait in her bedroom tower for morning to come.

Obi awoke with a start. She sat bolt upright. Blinking, she peered all about her. It was daylight out! How could it be daylight out? She must've fallen asleep! She hadn't meant to fall asleep! She had planned to stay up all night and sneak out of her cage at the crack of dawn before Rachel was awake and climb into Rachel's backpack to read her homework paper.

Obi glanced over at Rachel's bunk bed. Rachel was not in her bed! Nor was she anywhere in the room! Where was she? Oh, no, Rachel hadn't gone off to school already, had she? If Rachel had, how would Obi get to read her homework paper? How would she find out who Rachel wrote about? She wouldn't! Obi would spend the rest of her life having doubts, always tormented, always wondering if she was Rachel's favorite pet!

Then Obi realized something. Rachel's blue back-pack was still on the bedroom floor! So Rachel had not gone to school yet! She was probably just down-stairs, eating breakfast!

Obi wasted no time. She glanced over at Wan's cage. The little gerbil was hidden beneath a big mound of cedar shavings, still sound asleep. Wan did not know that Obi knew how to escape from her cage, and she didn't want him finding out now. Obi scrambled down her tube. She scurried over to the front of her cage and rose up onto her hind legs. Ever so gently and quietly, Obi pushed open the square cage door with her two front paws, and climbed out of her cage. Being careful not to wake Wan, Obi crept across the

dresser to the lamp that sat in the corner. Unlike Mr.
Durkins, Obi did not leap off the dresser: she chose
the more conventional route of sliding
down the lamp cord.

The moment she was on the
carpet, Obi dashed over to
Rachel's backpack. The main
compartment of Rachel's backpack
was unzipped. Obi climbed in. She spotted the paper
right away. It was on top of one of Rachel's textbooks.
The paper was written in Rachel's unmistakable, very
neat and easy-to-read handwriting. The paper was
titled:

My Favorite Pet

Obi took a deep breath and, trembling, started to
read.

"I have three pets . . ." Rachel had begun her paper.
"Two gerbils and a—"

Just then, behind her, Obi heard a sound—a *ziiiip*!
Obi's heart all but stopped! Startled, she spun about

just in time to see the zipper on the backpack close! Her eyes widened in horror! She gasped!

"No! NO! *NO!!*" Obi cried out in alarm, rushing toward the zipper. "I'm in here, Mom! I'm in your backpack! Don't zip me in!"

Obi now found herself in total darkness, trapped inside Rachel's backpack! It didn't take long for Obi to figure out what must be happening. Having finished breakfast, Rachel had come upstairs and, not knowing Obi was snooping around inside her backpack (why would she?), she zipped it up! Obi felt a sudden jerk as the backpack was lifted up into the air! The gerbil lost her footing and tumbled backward onto a small calculator. Obi thought her heart would explode, it was now beating so fast.

Rachel was taking her to school!

Chapter Three Off to School

Obi had never been so frightened in all her life. She didn't know what to do! Actually, there really wasn't much she could do! It was dark and cramped inside the nylon backpack, without much space for Obi to move around.

Rachel was a student who really liked to cram stuff into her backpack. In addition to quite a number of school textbooks, it was chock-full with spiral-bound notebooks (in all different sizes), pencils (some with very sharp points), pens, stray paper clips, a little plastic pencil sharpener, a plastic ruler, a rubber eraser, a calculator, several rubber bands, an apple juice pack, elastic hair ties, a plastic comb, a crumpled Band-Aid that was still in its wrapper, a pack of chewing gum, an unopened snack pack of apple sauce, and a smooshed granola bar! And those were only *some* of the things in the backpack. It was amazing the girl could carry all this stuff!

No wonder whenever Obi saw Rachel come into her bedroom with her backpack strapped on her back, she walked all stooped over, like she had the weight of the world on her shoulders! She practically did! Plus, little did Rachel know, but she now carried the weight of a small gerbil, too!

All at once, Obi felt the backpack start to bounce up and down. To steady herself, Obi grabbed hold of the nearest thing she saw. The nearest thing turned out to be an empty box of animal crackers. The backpack was really bouncing about! What was Rachel doing? Then Obi realized Rachel was hurrying down the stairs to the first floor of her house.

"Bye, Mom!" Obi heard Rachel cry out when she got downstairs.

"Do you have your lunch?" Mrs. Armstrong asked.

"Oh, my gosh! No, I don't!"

Obi felt Rachel's step quicken as the girl hurried into the kitchen. Suddenly, Obi felt the backpack swing through the air. There was a loud *THUMP*! as the backpack slammed onto the kitchen counter. Obi, blinking, felt all dizzy from the jolt. Just then, above her, Obi saw the zipper start to slide open. Quickly, frantically, she scrambled into the empty animal cracker box. The last thing Obi wanted was for Rachel to discover her snooping around in her backpack.

Peeking out from inside the box, Obi saw the bottom of a blue cloth lunch bag as it was being shoved into the backpack. Then Obi heard the zipper zip close. Obi sighed. That was a close one! Obi felt the backpack being lifted up into the air. Rachel was on the move again.

Obi sniffed. What was that horrible smell? Whatever it was, it stunk to high heavens! It smelled just like . . .

OH, NO! Obi groaned as she realized what it smelled like.

Cat's breath! It smelled just like cat's breath! That is, cat's breath after one of the Armstrongs' three cats—Sweetie Smoochkins, Sugar Smacks, or Honey Buns—had eaten a can of tuna cat food and then come upstairs to visit Obi in her cage!

Rachel had a tuna fish sandwich for lunch! It was inside her cloth lunch bag! Of all the days Obi had to sneak into Rachel's backpack, she *had* to pick a day that Rachel was having a tuna fish sandwich for lunch!

"Good-bye, Mom!" Obi heard Rachel call out to her mother.

"Bye, dear!" Mrs. Armstrong replied. "Have a great day at school!"

Rachel opened the front door. Before she stepped outside, though, Obi felt Rachel bend down.

"Bye-bye, Kenobi! You be a good dog while I'm at school, okay?"

Obi felt so envious that Rachel had said good-bye and petted Kenobi! Rachel hadn't said good-bye and petted Obi before going off to school! It was a good thing she hadn't, of course, since she would've found Obi gone from her cage. But *still!*

Obi heard the front door close behind her. Rachel

was outside the house now. And walking fast! Even though Obi couldn't see where Rachel was going, she knew. Each school day morning, Obi would peer out of the window that was beside Rachel's dresser (and Obi's cage) and watch as her adoptive mother walked down the road to wait at the corner with a bunch of other kids. After a while, a big yellow human mobile would appear from down another road. A stop sign on the side of the human mobile would flip out, red lights would start to flash, and the vehicle would stop and pick Rachel and the other students up to take them to school.

As Rachel was walking to the corner, Obi decided she needed a plan. She needed to figure out how she was going to get through this day without Rachel discovering her.

Fortunately, Obi thought of something in a matter of moments. She would do nothing—nothing at all! She would simply hide out in Rachel's backpack and do her best to avoid being caught. As soon as Rachel returned home from school that afternoon, Obi would sneak out of the backpack and hurry back into her cage. Admittedly, it would be a rather long day spent in a dark, cramped backpack, but Obi thought she could handle it. That was assuming, of course, she didn't keel over from all the horrid tuna fish fumes!

Chapter Four

A New World

To Obi's surprise, she found she was actually kind of excited about being a stowaway in Rachel's backpack. That's not to say she wasn't extremely nervous and anxious. She was! She also felt a little queasy, thanks to Rachel's smelly tuna fish sandwich. But she was also on an adventure and that excited Obi! She had never been to school before. She had no idea what went on there. It would be thrilling, she thought, to find out. True, she'd be stuck inside a backpack all day, but that still beat being stuck inside a cage all day.

There was something else Obi was looking forward to. It was something that, admittedly, was kind of sneaky. Hidden inside Rachel's backpack, Obi would be able to listen in on Rachel's conversations. Obi could be a spy—like *Harriet the Spy*! She could be

Obi the Spy! Of all the books that Mr. Armstrong had read aloud to Rachel, *Harriet the Spy* was one of Obi's all-time favorites!

"Hi, Rachel!" Obi heard a girl's voice say.

"Oh, hi, Grace!" Obi heard Rachel answer back. Obi knew who Grace was: she was Rachel's best friend. Grace's family lived down the road from the Armstrongs. Rachel and Grace often played together after school and on the weekends. "How are you today?"

"Good!" replied Grace. "And you?"

"Good!"

"That's good!"

"What did you do last night?"

"Not much. What about you?"

"Not much."

So far this wasn't exactly the most thrilling conversation Obi had ever heard, at least not from a spy's point of view. But then Grace said something that caused Obi's ears to perk up.

"So, Rach, I'm dying to find out. Which of your three pets did you write about for your homework paper?"

Obi became very still. And nervous. She was about

to learn who Rachel had said was her favorite pet.

"Who did *you* write about?" Rachel asked.

"No, you first!"

"No, you!"

"But I asked you *first*!"

"I'm not telling you until you tell me!"

"Okay, okay!" said Grace. "I wrote about my hamster. Now your turn. Who did you say was your favorite pet?"

"I wrote about—oh, no, look who's coming! Cleo!"

As Rachel said this, she groaned. Clearly, she did not care for whoever this Cleo was. And to be perfectly honest, neither did Obi! The gerbil had been all set to find out who Rachel's favorite pet was, and Cleo had to come along and interrupt things!

"How much do you want to bet she's going to tell us how horrible she did on her homework assignment last night?" Rachel said to Grace.

"And then she'll end up getting an A," said Grace.

"Try an A plus!"

It was then that Obi realized she knew who Cleo was. She'd heard Rachel and Grace talk about Cleo in Rachel's bedroom. Neither girl cared much for Cleo.

From what Obi was able to make out, Cleo was the brightest student in class, always getting A's. But rather than keep that to herself, Cleo let everyone know she always got A's—or, at least, she always let Rachel and Grace know. What *really* annoyed Rachel and Grace, though, was that Cleo always acted shocked when she got an excellent grade. Like it was a huge surprise to her!

"Hey, guys," said a new voice, a girl's voice, a girl's chirpy voice. Obi decided this must be Cleo. "How'd you do on the homework paper Mrs. Creesy gave us to write? The one about our favorite pet?"

"It went okay," replied Rachel in a very noncommittal sort of way.

"Really?" said Cleo. "You didn't have trouble writing it? Oh, my gosh! I had so much trouble writing mine! I wrote about my cat, Theo, but I couldn't figure out what to write about. Theo is such an amazing pet, I found it impossible to pick only a few things to write about! I just know I got a really bad grade on my paper!"

"Oh, I'm sure you did better than you think you did," Grace said.

"I don't think so," said Cleo.

"You always say that!"

"Oh, look! Here comes the school bus!" said Rachel.

Obi thought she detected a note of relief in Rachel's voice, like she was glad that the school bus had arrived. To be honest, Obi felt the exact same way. She had heard enough about Cleo's "amazing" cat, Theo! As far as Obi was concerned, there was no such thing as an amazing cat! Only *really* annoying cats!

From inside Rachel's backpack, Obi heard the loud rumble of what sounded like an enormous human mobile. Then she heard the squeal of squeaky brakes as it slowed to a stop, and then the sound of a door unfolding open. It was at this point that Obi realized something. The sounds she was hearing were being made by the big human mobile that Obi saw each school day morning from Rachel's bedroom window. What did Rachel say it was called? A school bus? Yes, that was it: a school bus!

"Good morning!" Obi heard a woman's cheerful voice call out. Obi decided this voice must belong to the driver of the school bus.

Rachel's backpack began jiggling up and down

again as Rachel climbed aboard the school bus and walked down the aisle. Obi heard a boy's voice call out, "Hey, Rachel! Hey, Grace!"

"Hi, Liam!" both girls responded.

Obi felt Rachel pull off her backpack and plop down in a seat, placing her backpack on her lap. Then Obi heard Grace sit down beside Rachel. Then Obi heard Liam in the seat in front of them say, "Look what I got!" He sounded very excited.

"What *is* that?"

"It's a fake ice cube!"

"I can see that," said Rachel. "What's that *in* the center of it?"

"A dead fly!" replied Liam, and chuckled.

"A dead *fly*?" said Grace.

"Yeah! It's a fake ice cube with a dead fly stuck in it!"

"Oh, no, Liam, you're not planning to—"

"Oh, yes I am!" There was a mischievous tone in Liam's voice.

"Liam, you know what happened the last time you tried to play a joke on other kids in school," Rachel said. "It backfired! It only got you in lots of trouble!"

"Not this time!" said Liam. "*This* time is going to be different!"

"That's what you always say!"

"No! Not always!"

"Well, just make sure Mrs. Creesy doesn't catch you with it in class," warned Rachel. "You know what *she'll* do!"

Obi was very curious to find out what Mrs. Creesy would do, but, evidently, both Liam and Grace knew because neither one asked.

It was so noisy inside the vehicle, what with the loud rumble of the motor, plus all the chattering of kids, Obi had trouble hearing. After a while, she gave up trying to listen. The truth was, she was beginning to feel motion sickness. The school bus kept making frequent stops to pick up more students. And the smell of Rachel's tuna fish sandwich wasn't helping matters, either. The last thing Obi wanted was to get sick inside her adoptive mother's back-pack! Obi decided she'd best just sit still, close her eyes, and try not to breathe in the tuna fish fumes.

And, of course, try not to be sick.

After a while, the school bus stopped making stops. It drove for what must've been a mile or so, then slowed down and made what felt like a sharp turn. A few moments later, the school bus came to a stop and its motor was turned off. Obi felt a sudden jerk as Rachel, getting up to leave, picked up her backpack and swung it over her shoulder.

"Watch your step getting off!" Obi heard the driver say to the students as they stepped off the bus.

Obi felt much better now that she was off the school bus. She was dying to see where Rachel was heading. Obi could hear Rachel, Grace, and Liam chatting as they walked. They must be outside the school now, Obi decided. Oh, if only she could see it, she thought.

Peering up, Obi spied a small opening in the zipper of the backpack. There was a hint of blue sky in the narrow opening. Obi hopped out of the animal cracker box and climbed up onto the top of Rachel's cloth

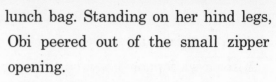

lunch bag. Standing on her hind legs, Obi peered out of the small zipper opening.

Unfortunately, since the backpack was on Rachel's back, all Obi could see was what was behind Rachel, not where Rachel, Grace, and Liam were heading. Obi saw school buses lined up alongside the curb of a cement plaza and a lot of kids getting off the buses and walking in the same direction as Rachel, Grace, and Liam were, but that was about it.

But then a very unexpected thing happened. Obi heard Liam cry out, "Think fast!" Then, to Obi's surprise, she saw a small object sail through the air. It whizzed right past Obi's head! It looked just like—well, just like an ice cube! *Wait!* It *was* an ice cube! The ice cube hit the ground and skipped across the concrete surface of the plaza. It was only after it came to a stop that Obi saw that there was a little speck in the center of the ice cube.

A somewhat pudgy boy with longish brown hair suddenly appeared from behind Obi. He was wearing faded jeans and a blue hoodie. He headed straight toward the ice cube.

Could this be Liam, Obi wondered?

"Who taught *you* how to catch?" the boy said, glancing over his shoulder.

"Who taught *you* to throw something at someone who's not looking?" replied Rachel as she and Grace both swung around to see the boy. "I'm telling you, Liam, you're going to lose that fake ice cube if you aren't more careful!"

So *this* was Liam!

Rachel only turned around for a split second to watch Liam pick up the ice cube, but that was enough. In that brief moment, Obi saw where Rachel, Grace, and Liam were heading. They were on their way into a large, brick, two-story building that had a flat roof and rows of large classroom windows.

They were heading into school!

As Rachel, Grace, and Liam entered the main entrance of the building, Obi was very aware of her heart pounding excitedly inside her chest.

She felt like she had just entered a new world!

Chapter Five

A Change of Plans

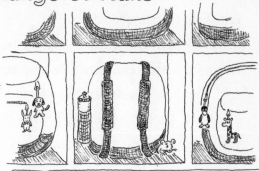

Risky though it was, Obi couldn't resist peeking out of the little zipper opening in Rachel's backpack as Rachel walked through the school hallway. Obi stared in fascination at all the kids she saw. There were so many of them! Boys. Girls. Tall kids. Short kids. Skinny kids. Not so skinny kids. Kids with long hair. Kids with short hair. Black kids. White kids. Brown kids. Asian kids. Kids with blond, brown, black, or red hair—one kid even had a blue streak in her hair! Kids walking with other kids. Kids walking alone. Kids talking. Kids laughing. Kids being goofy. Kids being serious. Kids carrying backpacks. Kids pulling backpacks with little wheels along the floor. Kids with their mothers. Kids with their fathers. It was all sheer pandemonium and, frankly, extremely noisy!

Suddenly, Obi heard a loud bell go off. The bell rang for about ten seconds and then went quiet. The bell had the most curious effect on the students. All of them, including Rachel, Grace, and Liam, began rushing to get to their classrooms.

Evidently, Rachel, Grace, and Liam all had Mrs. Creesy as their fourth-grade teacher. Her classroom was down at the end of the hallway. As they entered the room, Rachel pulled off her backpack and flung it into a cubby that was in a row of cubbies by the door. Obi, who had been standing on Rachel's lunch bag, was caught by surprise. She lost her balance and tumbled onto the lunch bag.

The weight of her small gerbil body caused the flap of the lunch bag to collapse inward, like a sprung trapdoor. Obi plunged into the lunch bag! She landed on top of Rachel's tuna fish sandwich—which was only

loosely wrapped up in a napkin! No wonder it was so smelly! The sandwich wasn't even wrapped in aluminum foil or plastic wrap! Quickly, her heart thumping furiously, Obi scrambled out of the lunch bag.

All at once, the inside of Rachel's backpack became inundated with tuna fish fumes! Obi thought the odor had been bad before, well, now it was ten times worse! The stench was overpowering! By falling into Rachel's lunch bag, Obi had let the trapped tuna fish fumes escape into the rest of the backpack. Obi felt like she was in the backpack with all three Armstrong cats when they had really bad tuna fish breath! There was no way Obi could spend the rest of the school day in Rachel's backpack, not with this horrible stinky odor! She had to get out of there—*now!*

Standing on Rachel's science textbook and using both her front paws, Obi grabbed hold of the zipper tab and pulled. The opening in the zipper grew bigger. Not much bigger but a little. Obi gave the zipper tab another yank. The opening grew a little bit bigger. Obi tugged again.

It wasn't long before the opening was big enough for Obi to squeeze through. She crawled out and slid down Rachel's backpack, past the menagerie of little stuffed animal key chains that dangled from zippers on Rachel's backpack. Obi grabbed hold of a hippo key chain and used it to drop down onto the bottom of Rachel's small square cubby.

Being ever so cautious, Obi peeked out from behind the blue backpack. She saw Rachel and about twenty other students seated at desks with their backs turned to Obi. The desks were grouped together like islands. A thin, middle-aged woman with black hair that had streaks of gray in it stood in front of the students, talking to them. She had a very serious look on her face—she looked like someone who did not tolerate a lot of silliness. This must be Rachel's teacher, Obi decided—Mrs. Creesy.

"While we're waiting for the principal to give her morning announcements, I'd like to collect everyone's homework papers," Mrs. Creesy announced. She began walking about the classroom, collecting each student's homework. "I hope you all had fun writing about your favorite pet."

Quite a number of kids, including Rachel, had left their homework papers in their backpacks. Obi gasped in horror when she saw Rachel get up and start to head for her cubby. Terrified that she was about to be discovered, Obi leaped behind Rachel's backpack, breathing hard. She had to hide, but *where*?

Glancing about, Obi noticed that the little outside pocket on Rachel's backpack was partially unzipped. Quickly, Obi scrambled in just as Rachel got to her cubby. As Obi scrunched down into the pocket (which seemed to be mostly filled with pennies), she heard Rachel unzip the main part of the backpack. Then she heard Rachel rummage around inside the backpack. (Obi certainly was glad she had gotten out of *that* part of the backpack!) Obi heard the zipper zip up again. Obi waited until she was certain Rachel was back at her desk. Then, ever so quietly, she crept out of her hiding spot and poked her head out from behind the backpack.

"Good morning, students!" a woman's cheerful voice suddenly boomed out from—well, Obi wasn't sure quite where the voice was coming from. The voice seemed to be coming from everywhere! *Who* was talking? It wasn't Mrs. Creesy—unless she knew how to talk without moving her lips! So whose voice was this?

"This is Ms. Pearson, your principal! Before I lead you in the Pledge of Allegiance, I'd like to wish the following students a very happy birthday!" As the principal began to read the names of students whose birthdays it was that day, Obi realized the voice was coming from a round speaker that was built into the classroom ceiling.

While the class listened to the principal make her morning announcements, Obi kept her eyes on Mrs. Creesy. By now, she had collected all of the homework papers. She brought them to her desk, which was at the back of the room, near the classroom window. Obi watched as Mrs. Creesy put the papers in a blue folder on top of her desk, and then went to the chalkboard.

Mrs. Creesy waited until the principal had finished her morning announcements and the students had all said the Pledge of Allegiance. Then she said, "Today we're going to continue where we left off yesterday on learning about the Oregon Trail. Now, who remembers what years the Oregon Trail took place?"

While Mrs. Creesy looked about the classroom trying to decide which student to call on, Obi's gaze fell upon the blue folder of homework papers. She suddenly changed her mind about hanging out in Rachel's cubby all day and came up with a new plan. It was a risky plan, fraught with peril, but Obi felt she really had no choice—she would just have to do it.

While Mrs. Creesy stood at the chalkboard, talking about the Oregon Trail, the little gerbil slipped out from behind the backpack in Rachel's cubby. Quietly, stealthily, she dropped down to the linoleum-tiled floor. Keeping close to the wall, Obi scurried across the floor to Mrs. Creesy's desk. There, she stopped under the desk to regain her composure and wait for her wildly pounding heart to calm down a bit.

When it was clear that her heart was not going to settle down, Obi continued with her plan. Turning, she saw an electrical cord dangling down the side of Mrs. Creesy's desk. Obi stepped over to the cord, took hold of it in her two front paws, and began to climb. In no time at all, she reached the top of Mrs. Creesy's desk. As she pulled herself up onto the desk,

Obi saw that the cord was to an electric pencil sharpener. Obi glanced over at Mrs. Creesy and very nearly had a heart attack! Mrs. Creesy had turned from the chalkboard and was now facing her students—and her desk! Terrified that she was out in the open, in plain view on Mrs. Creesy's desk, Obi leaped behind the electric pencil sharpener where the teacher could not see her.

Obi's whole body was shaking; she was so nervous. Obi peeked out from behind the pencil sharpener and gave a sigh of relief. Mrs. Creesy once again was writing on the chalkboard, with her back turned.

The teacher had not seen her!

Obi waited a moment before making her next move, before darting over to the blue folder. That was her plan, to go to the blue folder, open it, and read Rachel's homework. It was—no question about it—an extremely dangerous thing to do. It was also an ex-

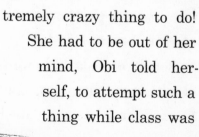

tremely crazy thing to do! She had to be out of her mind, Obi told herself, to attempt such a thing while class was in session! But she *had* to do it! She *had* to find out who Rachel's favorite pet was! Obi could not go home without finding out who Rachel had written about! She just couldn't! After all, wasn't that the whole reason why she was in this mess?

Obi was about to creep over to the blue folder when her gaze fell upon two boys whose desks were in the back of the classroom. One of the boys was Liam.

The reason Obi noticed them was because neither boy was paying any attention to Mrs. Creesy. Liam, who sat between Rachel and this other boy, was showing something to the boy. It was the fake ice cube with the dead fly in it! Liam looked like he was trying to be very secretive, keeping his hands below his desk so Mrs. Creesy wouldn't be able to see the fake ice cube. The problem was Liam's face. He was grinning like a maniac. At one point, Obi noticed Rachel, her eyes focused straight ahead on Mrs. Creesy, give Liam a sharp poke on the arm with her elbow, to warn him to be careful.

But really, this wasn't any of Obi's concern. All Obi cared about was getting to that blue folder and read-

ing Rachel's homework paper. That was it! Well, that and making sure she made it through the day without being caught, of course!

Gathering up her courage, Obi started to make her move toward the blue folder. She had just reached the blue folder when she glanced toward the chalkboard to check up on Mrs. Creesy. Obi froze in her tracks. Mrs. Creesy was staring at the back of the classroom—where Obi was—with a very vexed look on her face! But it wasn't Obi that her eyes were fixed upon—it was Liam!

As Mrs. Creesy continued to talk about the Oregon Trail, the teacher slowly made her way to the back of the classroom. Students turned in their seats to watch Mrs. Creesy as she walked past them. Liam and the other boy were so busy looking at the fake ice cube, neither one noticed Mrs. Creesy until she was practically hovering over them. But by then, it was too late. By then, the frown on Mrs. Creesy's face had turned into a very disapproving scowl. By then, too, Obi had darted back to her hiding spot behind the electronic pencil sharpener.

"What have you got there, Liam?" Mrs. Creesy asked.

Liam practically leaped out of his chair he was so startled. "Uh, nothing!" he nervously blurted out as he quickly shoved the fake ice cube into his pants pocket.

Mrs. Creesy held out her hand, palm up. "I'll take that, thank you!"

"But—" exclaimed Liam.

"You know the rules, Liam," Mrs. Creesy said in a firm voice that left no room for dispute. "When you're in my class, I want your undivided attention."

"But—"

"Please give it to me, Liam!"

Liam looked crestfallen. With a forlorn sigh, he reached into his pocket and pulled out the fake ice cube with the dead fly in it. He surrendered it into Mrs. Creesy's outstretched hand.

"Oh, for goodness sake!" Mrs. Creesy muttered when she saw what Liam had given her.

As Mrs. Creesy turned away from Liam, Obi nearly let out a shriek. Instead of returning to the chalkboard, which was what Obi had expected Mrs. Creesy to do, she was coming toward her desk—toward Obi!

Obi tried not to panic. She tried to keep her wits about her. Mrs. Creesy was on her way to her desk, where Obi was hiding! Unless Mrs. Creesy was as blind as a bat, she was sure to notice a little gerbil cowering behind her electric pencil sharpener. Not only that, but Mrs. Creesy did not look happy! Evidently, finding one of her students with a fake ice cube had put her in a really bad mood. What would Mrs. Creesy do when she found out she had a gerbil on her desk, too? Would she go ballistic?

Obi wasn't about to find out!

Frantic, Obi glanced about for someplace else to hide. But *where*?

Obi noticed that one of the drawers in Mrs. Creesy's desk was slightly open. The drawer was close to where Obi crouched behind the electric pencil sharpener. Without giving it a second thought, Obi dashed over and dove into the desk drawer.

She landed on a box of cough drops, spilling a few out. It was so dark inside the drawer, Obi could scarcely see. As she scooted to the back of the drawer, she bumped into something, then something else. Then she knocked into something that made a feeble buzzing noise, like the sound she once heard a trapped wasp make as its wings bumped against the inside of Rachel's bedroom window. Obi came to a flat, rubbery pancake-shaped thing. She had no idea what it was. Obi stopped. She was breathing hard and her heart was pounding fast. With no idea where to go next, Obi slipped under the rubbery pancake thing. She did so just in the nick of time.

All at once, the most terrifying thing happened. The desk drawer flung open! Obi froze! Thank goodness she was under the rubbery pancake thing and out of sight! Obi did not move a muscle, not a whisker!

Now that the drawer had been pulled open, everything in it

was visible—including, Obi realized to her horror, her long, spindly tail! Her tail was sticking out in plain sight! Obi was about to yank her tail in when, out of the corner of her eye, just beyond the round edge of the rubbery pancake thing, she saw Mrs. Creesy's hand! She wore red fingernail polish, and she was holding the fake ice cube that she had taken from Liam. Obi held her breath as Mrs. Creesy's hand dropped the ice cube into the desk drawer. Obi was sure Mrs. Creesy would spot her tail. The gerbil braced herself, expecting Mrs. Creesy to let out a startled gasp. Or a bloodcurdling scream. But Mrs. Creesy did neither. No, she made no sound whatsoever! Evidently, Obi's tail must've blended in with everything else in the drawer. Mrs. Creesy's hand disappeared from Obi's view, and the desk drawer was pushed back in! Well, almost back in.

Obi slipped out from her hiding place. Because Mrs. Creesy had left the drawer slightly opened, some classroom light spilled into the drawer through the narrow opening. For the first time, Obi was able to see what the rubbery pancake thing was. Her mouth fell open. She was stunned! It was a whoopee cushion! Obi knew all about whoopee cushions—Craig, Rachel's older brother, had one. He got a big kick out of blowing air into it and then sneaking into Rachel's bedroom and hiding it on Rachel's desk chair. He would then laugh uproariously when Rachel unwittingly sat down on the whoopee cushion, causing it to issue a loud, explosive fart noise.

Obi was absolutely dumbfounded. What on earth was Mrs. Creesy doing with a whoopee cushion in her desk drawer? She didn't seem like the kind of teacher who would think it was funny to put a whoopee cushion on one of her student's chairs.

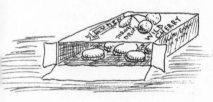

Then it dawned on Obi what this desk drawer must be. This was where Mrs. Creesy put all the things she confiscated from her students who were playing with or eating things in class that they shouldn't have been. Obi felt like she had stumbled upon a cave of naughty student treasures. In addition to the whoopee cushion and the box of cough drops, Obi could make out a squirt gun, a windup plastic toad that flipped when you wound it up (which must have been what

Obi heard buzzing), an opened
pack of chewing gum, an electronic
handheld game, a box of Dots, a small
rubber super ball, a joy buzzer (another gag Craig loved
to play on Rachel),
a compass, and, now,
Liam's fake ice cube with the dead
fly in it.

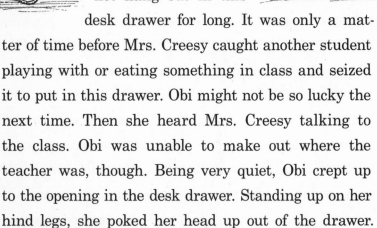

Obi knew she could
not hang out in this
desk drawer for long. It was only a mat-
ter of time before Mrs. Creesy caught another student
playing with or eating something in class and seized
it to put in this drawer. Obi might not be so lucky the
next time. Then she heard Mrs. Creesy talking to
the class. Obi was unable to make out where the
teacher was, though. Being very quiet, Obi crept up
to the opening in the desk drawer. Standing up on her
hind legs, she poked her head up out of the drawer.
She gasped and ducked back down.

Mrs. Creesy was standing less than a foot away,
talking to the class!

Obi, trembling, scurried to the back of the desk drawer, where she couldn't be seen. The little gerbil tried to think of what to do. Well, one thing she could do, she told herself, was to stop being so darn reckless! What was she *thinking* climbing up onto Mrs. Creesy's desk while class was in session!? Obi vowed that, from here on out, she was going to be much more cautious. That was assuming, of course, she ever got out of this desk drawer. Just when Obi was beginning to think that Mrs. Creesy would never leave her desk, Obi heard Mrs. Creesy walking away. Curious, Obi got up, crept to the front of the drawer, and peeked out. Sure enough, Mrs. Creesy was now on the other side of the classroom, by the chalkboard.

Quickly, Obi crawled out onto the lip of the drawer. She was about to drop down to the floor when she noticed something. Mrs. Creesy's desk was only about a foot or so away from the large classroom window. The window had a wide ledge. There were

all sorts of fascinating things on the ledge—a large papier-mâché volcano, exotic potted plants, a globe of the earth, a small model of a human skeleton (which Obi found rather creepy), and a miniature covered wagon, which had a little cardboard sign leaning against it that said OREGON TRAIL COVERED WAGON.

Obi got up on her hind legs, took a quick glance around to make sure nobody was looking in her direction, saw that nobody was, and sprang. She landed on the window ledge, near the earth globe. Moving fast, Obi hid under the earth globe, below the South Pacific Ocean and Antarctica.

For the rest of that morning, Obi hung out under the globe. She just sat there, biding her time, listening to Mrs. Creesy talk about the Oregon Trail. Every so often Obi glanced over at Rachel, curious to see what her adoptive mother was doing. The girl sat at her desk, sometimes doodling on her notepad, sometimes gazing up at Mrs. Creesy with the most absorbed look on her face. Rachel would be so shocked, Obi thought, if she knew that her pet gerbil (or one of them, at any rate) was in the classroom right that moment, too, listening and learning, just like she was!

By and by, the history lesson ended. Mrs. Creesy instructed her students to take out their math books. As they did so, Mrs. Creesy began talking about decimals. Obi had really enjoyed hearing about the Oregon Trail, but, in all honesty, she found decimals a bit dry for her taste. She just couldn't seem to get into them. She tried—she did—but her mind drifted. So did her eyes. She found herself gazing up at the earth globe that hovered above her, like a huge disco ball. She wondered what it would be like to live in Antarctica. Did gerbils even live in Antarctica? If they did, Obi wondered how they liked living at the bottom of the earth.

When Obi wasn't peering over at Rachel or gazing up at Antarctica, she stared out the classroom window. Frankly, it was hard not to. For one thing, it was a gorgeous spring day out, with lots of blue sky and bright sun. Plus, Mrs. Creesy's window looked out onto the school playground, where some kids were running around, playing tag. They were laughing and screaming, and they looked like they were all having a blast. It was hard not to be distracted by them!

As the morning wore on, Obi began to grow drowsy.

The late morning sun, which was shining in through the classroom window, was beating down upon her. It felt so warm and cozy. Obi struggled to keep awake, but her eyelids grew heavier and heavier. At one point, Obi must've dozed off because, suddenly, she was jolted awake by the sound of a loud ringing bell.

Obi's eyes flew open. For a moment, she had no idea where she was. Then she saw the classroom and remembered. To Obi's surprise, all the students, including Rachel, were getting up from their desks and leaving the classroom.

"Lunchtime!" Obi heard one boy cry out excitedly as he jumped up from his desk by the window.

"Thank goodness!" said another boy who sat at the same group of desks. "I'm *starving*!"

The next thing Obi knew, all the students, including Rachel, were gone. Obi was all alone in the classroom with Mrs. Creesy. It felt strange and eerily quiet being in the classroom with only Mrs. Creesy.

With all her students off at lunch, Obi wondered what Mrs. Creesy would do next. Would she, too, go to lunch? If she did, Obi knew what *she* would do next. She would sneak back onto Mrs. Creesy's desk and take a peek inside that blue folder and read Rachel's homework paper.

Much to Obi's disappointment, though, Mrs. Creesy went to the front of the classroom and began to erase the chalkboard.

Wasn't Mrs. Creesy hungry? Didn't she want to go eat lunch, too? Wasn't she sick of being in the classroom? Didn't she want to get a change of scenery?

Obi heard a tap on the classroom door. She turned and saw a tall, skinny man with bushy hair standing in the doorway. He wore glasses and had on a navy blue jacket and the most hideous-looking tie. The tie, which was a bright canary yellow, had little cartoon drawings of cat faces printed all over it. It had to be the *ugliest* tie Obi had ever seen!

"Hey, Marge," the man said, smiling. Since he seemed to be on a first name basis with Mrs. Creesy, Obi decided he must be another teacher. "You up for a bite to eat in the teachers' lounge?"

Mrs. Creesy put down the chalk eraser, smiled, and said, "You bet I am!"

Obi watched as Mrs. Creesy stepped away from the chalkboard. Instead of walking to the door, though, Mrs. Creesy went to her desk and, to Obi's dismay, picked up the blue folder with all the homework papers!

"I probably should get started on these homework papers while I'm at lunch," she said as she went to join the teacher with the ugly cat tie. "You know me— always got to be doing something."

The other teacher chuckled. "I sure do know you! You're one of the most dedicated teachers I know!"

Chapter Eight

Obi the Spy

Obi was not a gerbil who got fuming mad very often. But when Mrs. Creesy picked up the blue folder and left the classroom with it—well, that got Obi fuming mad! Now, all because Mrs. Creesy had to be so dedicated, Obi would not be able to read Rachel's homework paper while everyone was at lunch.

Obi tried to remember where the Ugly Cat Tie Teacher had said he and Mrs. Creesy were going. Obi had been so distracted by his horrid tie, she couldn't recall. Was it the teachers' scrounge? No, that wasn't it. The teachers' flounge? No, it wasn't that, either. Wait . . . the teachers' lounge—was that it? Yes, *that* was it! That was what he had said! The teachers' lounge! Obi wondered where the teachers' lounge could be. She also wondered if there might be an opportunity for her to read Rachel's homework paper in the teachers' lounge. Well, there was only one way to find out, wasn't there? And so, forgetting all about her vow to be more cautious, Obi hopped down off the window ledge and scurried across the linoleum-tiled floor to the classroom doorway.

The moment Obi stepped out into the school hallway, she stopped. Puzzled, she glanced first in one direction, then in the other. She had no idea which way to go, left or right. Obi tried to remember which way Mrs. Creesy and the Ugly Cat Tie Teacher had gone. She was pretty sure they had gone left. So Obi headed in that direction. She was hurrying down the hallway when, up on the wall, she saw a bulletin board filled with student drawings. The drawings were of things you'd find in space—planets, asteroids, meteors, meteorites, comets, weather satellites, spacecrafts, nebulae, a space telescope, moons, star clusters. Obi, who was a huge fan of the *Star Wars* movies, was hoping she might see something *Star Wars* related—a Jedi knight holding a light saber, for instance—but, alas, she did not.

Just past the bulletin board, Obi came to a classroom in session, with its door open. Obi stopped just before she got to the doorway, paused, then, heart racing, dashed past the doorway, hoping nobody in the classroom saw her. So far as Obi could tell, no one did.

As Obi continued on her way, she kept a sharp eye out for students as well as any teachers. Luckily, she didn't see anyone. That's not to say it was quiet, though. No—far from it! In fact, behind one door, Obi heard all kinds of loud commotion. She heard the sound of running feet, squeaky sneakers, a whistle blowing, excited shouts, shrieks. Could *this* be the teachers' lounge? Obi wondered. Having never been in a teachers' lounge, she had no idea what teachers did there. Just then, on the other side of the door, Obi heard a lot of laughing and clapping. Curious to find out what was going on, Obi slipped through the crack under the door.

The moment Obi came out on the other side, she knew she was not in the teachers' lounge. For one thing, she saw no teachers, just a lot of students. The only adult she saw was a short, squat woman who was dressed in shorts and an exercise polo shirt. It was the same sort of outfit Rachel's mother, Mrs. Armstrong, wore when she went off to the fitness center to work out. The woman was the one who was blowing the whistle. She was also doing a lot of yelling and clapping her hands at the students, rooting them on, telling them what to do. The kids were in two lines that faced each other. They were throwing a big, red, rubber ball at one another. Lifting her eyes, Obi gazed about the room. It was an enormous room with a very high ceiling and a glossy wood floor that had red and blue lines painted on it. Obi saw basketball hoops (like those she saw in the neighbor's driveway when she was looking out Rachel's bedroom window) mounted on the walls and climbing ropes that looped down from the ceiling.

Just then, out of the corner of her eye, Obi spotted a flash of red hurtling toward her through the air!

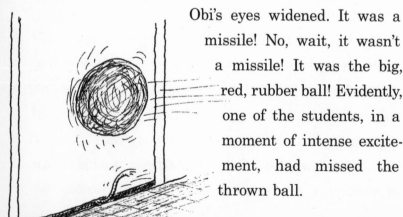

Obi's eyes widened. It was a missile! No, wait, it wasn't a missile! It was the big, red, rubber ball! Evidently, one of the students, in a moment of intense excitement, had missed the thrown ball.

Terrified, Obi shrieked! She spun about and darted back under the door just as the ball smashed against the door and bounced off.

Obi was so relieved to be back out in the hallway, where things were much calmer and safer. She turned and peered up at the door and saw there was a word printed on the wall beside the door. This room had a name: **GYMNASIUM**.

Suddenly, down the hallway, Obi heard loud voices and laughter—*kids'* loud voices and laughter! She turned and saw a bunch of students appear from around a corner, heading her way. Obi let out a startled gasp and, all in a panic, began to flee. Keeping close to the wall, she scurried down the hallway. Behind her, she heard the students getting closer. Obi came to a closed door and, heart thumping, slipped beneath it.

The room on the other side of the door was dimly lighted. Obi stopped and spun about. She waited, listening. Out in the hallway, she heard the students pass by. As their voices and laughter trailed off, Obi sighed.

BOOM-BOOM-BOOM! BA-BOOM-BA-BOOM-BA-BOOM!

Obi practically leaped out of her fur, she was so startled!

BOOM-BOOM-BOOM! BA-BOOM-BA-BOOM-BA-BOOM!

The thunderous sound came from behind Obi, from the room she was in. Obi had been in such a rush to get away from the students in the hallway, she hadn't even bothered to look around the darkened room she had entered. Obi whirled about and saw she was in a room filled with chairs that had music stands in front of them—like the music stand Rachel used in her bedroom when she practiced her violin. So far as Obi could see, only two humans were in the room—a boy and a girl. They were each standing in front of a huge kettledrum, with their backs to Obi, cheerfully pounding on the massive drums.

BA-BA-BOOM-BOOM! BA-BA-BOOM-BOOM! BA-BA-BOOM-BA-BOOM-BA-BOOM!

Obi had heard enough. Moving at lightning fast speed, she scooted back out under the door, into the hallway. She turned and peered up at the wall. This room was called **BAND ROOM**.

Obi made a mental note *never* go into the band room again! Continuing on her way, Obi soon came to another closed door. She lifted her eyes to see that this door was the room to **TEACHERS' LOUNGE**.

Obi stopped and stared at the door. She had found it! She had found the teachers' lounge! Behind this door was Rachel's homework paper! Well, Rachel's homework paper, plus Mrs. Creesy and the Ugly Cat Tie Teacher. Obi was so pleased with herself that she had tracked down Rachel's homework paper.

Obi the Jedi gerbil does it again!

Obi was about to squeeze under the teachers' lounge door when she caught a whiff of something delicious. It smelled like cheese! Melted cheese! Obi *loved* cheese! Either melted or unmelted! Obi breathed in the wonderful aroma, which seemed to be drifting from down the hallway. Obi, who considered herself to be something of a connoisseur on cheeses, had no trouble recognizing the cheese she smelled. It was yellow American cheese!

Suddenly curious, as well as incredibly hungry, Obi decided to investigate the smell. How could she not?

She didn't plan to venture far. Just down the hallway a bit, just until she saw where the melted-cheese smell was coming from. What was the harm in that?

Lured on by the delightful aroma, Obi heard what sounded like hundreds of students all talking at once farther down the hallway. The farther she went down the hallway, the louder the din became.

Obi came to a big open doorway that led into an enormous room that had enormous windows and rows and rows of long tables. Students were seated at the long tables, talking and eating. Obi peered up at the tiled wall and saw that this room, too, had a name, **CAFETERIA**.

Obi peered into the cafeteria. It sure smelled good in the cafeteria! As far as Obi was concerned, this was the best-smelling room in the entire school! The smell had a magical, hypnotic effect on Obi. She forgot where she was! In a dreamy daze, she wandered into the cafeteria!

And then it happened!

She ran into a student!

Not just any student! She ran into Rachel's friend, Liam!

Liam, who was holding a tray of food, had just stepped away from the counter where the utensils, napkins, ketchup, and mustard were all located. Liam spied Obi at the exact same moment Obi spied Liam. Both Obi and Liam stopped dead in their tracks. They both stared at each other, their eyes wide with shock.

Startled to have been spotted, Obi let out a horrified shriek!

Startled to spot a gerbil in the cafeteria, Liam let out a horrified shriek!

But that wasn't the only thing Liam did. He also dropped his cafeteria tray! It crashed onto the floor. His plate and utensils clattered on the tiled floor. Food splattered everywhere! That was when Obi saw what Liam was having for lunch: a grilled-cheese sandwich. So *that* was what Obi had smelled—grilled cheese!

Needless to say, Obi did not hang around to see if Liam was okay or help him clean up the mess. As she spun about to flee, Obi ran into another student—a skinny girl with long red hair—holding a tray. Her eyes bulged out and she shrieked, too! Then Obi heard heard more shrieks from other kids!

Terrified beyond belief, Obi took off as fast as she could out of the cafeteria and down the hallway. As she sped away, she heard Liam yell out: *"RAAAAAAAAAAT!"*

Chapter Nine

The worst Luck!

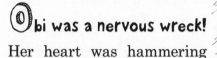

Obi was a nervous wreck! Her heart was hammering and her whole body was trembling. Her knees, all four of them, felt very wobbly! In a frantic state of mind, Obi ran like the blazes. She ran to the first door she saw. Just before scooting under the door, Obi glanced back at the cafeteria. Several students, including Rachel and Grace, had come over to help Liam pick up his tray and all the things that had been on it—plate, fork, spoon, knife, half-pint-sized carton of milk, straw, napkin, plus a little pudding bowl—off the floor. They were all crouched down, cleaning up the mess. Poor frazzled Liam was telling them all about the rat he had seen. He held out his hands to show how big the rat had been. He made Obi appear at least five times the size she really was!

Obi felt perfectly terrible that she had caused such mayhem. Luckily, everyone was so focused on Liam, nobody noticed Obi slip beneath the door.

The room Obi now found herself in was small, dark, and cramped. Straining her eyes to see in the shadowy light, Obi made out the smudgy forms of a metal pail, a push broom, a couple of mops, a number of cleaning products, and economy-sized packages of paper towels and toilet paper. Evidently, she was in some sort of supply closet!

Obi sat in the darkness and tried to calm down, but her heart just wouldn't stop racing. She was furious at herself for having been spotted. She was also furious at Liam. How *dare* he call her a rat! She didn't look anything at all like a rat! Gerbils are cute and cuddly; rats are, well, *rats*! They're pretty disgusting looking!

Obi was also furious at Mr. Durkins. If it wasn't for him, she'd be home in her cage right now, snuggled under a heap of cedar shavings, all safe and sound and happy. But, no, that sinister old mouse had to put doubts in Obi's mind, had to make her question who Rachel said was her favorite pet.

Just then, above her, Obi heard a key being inserted into the doorknob. Her heart practically stopped. Lifting her eyes, Obi saw the doorknob start to turn! Someone was coming into the supply closet! Someone must have seen her dart under the door!

Terrified, Obi jumped up and scurried behind the metal pail just as the door swung open. Light from the cafeteria hallway spilled into the closet. Quivering and nearly in tears from being so frightened, Obi peeked out from behind the pail and saw the outline of a tall, bald-headed man in the doorway. He reached into the closet and tugged on a string that dangled from a lightbulb that was attached to the ceiling. Instantly, the closet became flooded with light. Her heart thumping, Obi darted behind a big package of toilet paper. Now that the little room was filled with brilliant light, Obi saw that the man was wearing a gray uniform. He was the school janitor!

The janitor bent down and picked up the metal pail.

Good thing Obi had moved! The janitor also grabbed a mop. To Obi's astonishment—and huge relief—the janitor then stepped out of the supply closet. He disappeared down the hallway, leaving the door to the closet somewhat ajar.

As relieved as Obi was that she hadn't been caught, she knew she couldn't relax—not yet anyway. She was still a gerbil at large. She knew she had to get back to Mrs. Creesy's classroom—as fast as possible. Going to the teachers' lounge to try and read Rachel's homework paper was out of the question now.

Being very cautious, Obi crept out of the supply closet and peeked in the direction of the cafeteria. She was expecting to see Liam, Grace, and Rachel, but the only human she saw was the bald-headed janitor. He was mopping up the floor where Liam had dropped his cafeteria tray.

Obi turned and took off in the direction of Mrs. Creesy's classroom. She didn't get very far before she spotted another bunch of students coming toward her on their way to the cafeteria. Obi couldn't believe she'd run into more students! Where were they all coming from? Gosh, she sure was having the worst luck!

Obi glanced about for yet *another* place to hide! She saw a door that said BOYS on it. Obi had no idea why a door would say BOYS on it, nor, frankly, did she care—she needed a place to hide!

Obi hurried beneath the door and came out into a small, green-tiled room with two urinals, two bathroom stalls, and two sinks that were in front of a big, square mirror.

Oh, and a boy who stood in front of the sinks and mirror!

Obi froze and stared at the boy. The boy was leaning over so Obi couldn't see his face, just the top of his brown hair. He was using a wet paper towel to wipe some brown chocolaty stuff off his jeans.

Oh, no, it wasn't!

It was!

It was *Liam*!

Liam must've sensed someone was in the room besides him because he suddenly stopped wiping off his jeans. Slowly, slowly, he lifted his gaze. For the second time in less than a few minutes, Liam's eyes met Obi's. His face went ghastly pale and his mouth dropped open. For a long, anxious moment, Liam and Obi just stared at one another, each with a panicky, frightened look in their eyes.

This time, it was Liam who shrieked first.

"IT'S IN THE BOYS' ROOM! IT'S IN THE BOYS' ROOM!" he shouted hysterically as he dashed out of the boys' bathroom, into the hallway.

"IT'S IN THE BOYS' ROOM!" he cried out again, with a wild look in his eyes, as he raced down the hallway toward the cafeteria. He ran to the bald-headed janitor. Gasping for breath, Liam blurted out, "THE BOYS' ROOM! THE BOYS' ROOM! IT'S IN THE BOYS' ROOM!"

"Okay, Liam, take a deep breath and calm down," the janitor said. "Now tell me. What's in the boys' bathroom?"

"THE—THE—THE—THE—THE RAT!"

"You saw a rat?" the janitor said. He sounded skeptical, like he didn't quite believe Liam had actually seen a rat. "Let's you and I go take a look, shall we?"

Liam did not look too thrilled about having to go

back into the boys' bathroom. Still, he went. He did not lead the way, though—he let the janitor go first. Liam had a very apprehensive look on his face as he followed the janitor into the boys' bathroom.

But by then, Obi was long gone.

Obi just couldn't get a break! She really couldn't! She couldn't believe she had gone into a boys' bathroom and that Liam, of all boys, would be in there! Thank goodness all Liam was doing was wiping chocolate pudding off his pants!

As Obi raced down the hallway. She had tears in her eyes, she was so distraught! She hated being at school! Just hated it! She hated having to keep out of sight! It was so nerve-racking! All Obi wanted was to be back in her cage, snug in her cozy bedroom tower, nestled under a big pile of fragrant cedar shavings. But instead, here she was stuck in Rachel's school, alone and frightened, running all over the school, trying desperately not to be caught. And *why*? Because of Mr. Durkins, that's *why!* Why did that horrible old mouse have to tell her she may not be Rachel's favorite pet? Why? Why? *Why?*

Obi arrived at Mrs. Creesy's classroom and stopped in the doorway. She cautiously peeked in to see if Mrs. Creesy or anyone else was in the room. Nobody was. So Obi hurried in. She ran straight to the classroom window. Her plan was to climb up onto Mrs. Creesy's desk and, from there, hop onto the classroom window ledge, and then hide in the Oregon Trail covered wagon for the afternoon. She'd be safe in there, she thought, safe and out of sight.

There was just one problem. Mrs. Creesy's desk, which Obi needed to climb up onto to get to the window ledge, was no longer where it had been that morning! It was up in front of the classroom, by the chalkboard!

That's odd! thought Obi.

Glancing about the classroom, Obi noticed other strange things. The students' desks, for instance, were all arranged differently. And there were different things on the classroom walls.

Obi was totally bewildered. What was going on here?

Then, suddenly, Obi realized what was going on. She groaned and slapped her forehead. "Ugh!" she muttered, annoyed at herself.

No wonder everything looked so different! She was in the *wrong* classroom!

"Where are you supposed to be?" a voice behind Obi inquired. It was a deep, stern, harsh voice that seemed to come from, well, from up in the air.

Obi, startled, gasped and spun about and saw a small table. Tilting her head back, she saw a wire cage on top of the table. A large, furry, brown-and-white spotted guinea pig was in the cage, peering down at Obi.

"Oh! Hawo!" said Obi. She smiled up at the guinea pig. It wasn't much of a smile, though. The truth was, Obi was far too upset to give anyone a genuine smile.

Apparently, the guinea pig wasn't in a smiling mood, either. Not only did he not smile at Obi, he narrowed his eyes at her in what appeared to be a reprimanding sort of way.

"Where are you supposed to be right now, young lady?"

"Home!" replied Obi. She heard a quiver in her voice. Wow, she really was upset!

The guinea pig frowned at her. "Home? No, no! I mean whose class are you in?"

"I'm not in any class!"

Obi expected the guinea pig to show some sympathy when he heard this, particularly since her voice sounded like she was about to cry. But he didn't. No, in fact, if anything, he looked even more irritated. "Who's your teacher?"

"I don't have one!"

The guinea pig rolled his eyes. Clearly, Obi was trying his patience. He said, "You don't have a teacher?"

"No!"

The guinea pig sighed. "What grade are you in?"

"I'm not in any grade!"

For the first time, Obi thought she detected a slight look of compassion in the guinea pig's face. "You're new here, aren't you?" he asked.

"Yes! Yes, I am!"

"What's your name?"

"Obi!"

"Well, Obi, do you remember the name of the teacher whose classroom you were in before you came into this classroom?"

"Mrs. Creesy!"

The guinea pig nodded. "Okay, we can work with that!" he said. "Her classroom, in fact, is right next to this classroom. So you'd better get back there right now before you get caught. Otherwise, you're going to ruin it for all of us! You don't want to do that, do you?"

"No!" said Obi, shaking her head. "No, I don't!"

"Good! Well then, Obi, you'd better get that tail moving!" the guinea pig warned. "Lunchtime will be over any minute and—"

Before the guinea pig could finish what he was saying, the school bell rang.

The guinea pig's eyes widened in alarm. He became very frantic. "Lunchtime is over!" he cried. "All the fourth graders will be returning to their classrooms! Go on, get out of here! Fast! Get that tail moving, will ya, and get back to Mrs. Creesy's classroom! If you don't, you'll blow it for all of us!"

"I'm on my way!" exclaimed Obi.

And with that, Obi dashed out of the classroom and into Mrs. Creesy's classroom. It was empty. Obi ran across the linoleum-tiled floor and climbed up onto Mrs. Creesy's desk. From there, she took a running leap onto the window ledge and raced past the earth globe and exotic potted plants to the Oregon Trail covered wagon. Obi crawled into the back of the wagon and made herself comfortable under the white canopy. From the back of the covered wagon, Obi saw Mrs. Creesy enter the classroom. The teacher was holding the blue folder in her left hand. Obi watched as Mrs. Creesy set the blue folder down on her desk. By now, students had begun to return to the classroom. Obi spotted Rachel, Grace, and Liam enter the classroom. Liam still looked pretty shaken up. Well, he wasn't the only one! Obi was still pretty shaken up herself!

While Mrs. Creesy waited for her students to take their seats, Obi couldn't stop thinking about the guinea pig. She couldn't stop thinking about what he had said to her, before he told her to get her tail moving.

You'll blow it for all of us, he had said.

Blow *what* for all of them, and *who* was all of them? Obi wondered.

Chapter Eleven

On the Oregon Trail

As far as hiding places go, the little Oregon Trail covered wagon was a perfect place to hide. While Mrs. Creesy's class spent the afternoon going over science (the class was studying earthquakes), Obi hung out in the covered wagon and daydreamed.

She pretended that she was in a covered wagon on the Oregon Trail with Rachel's family. The Armstrongs were rolling across the hot, dusty prairie with all of their pets. The only one who wasn't with them was Mr. Durkins—Obi decided he was too evil to take on the Oregon Trail. Besides, he wasn't a pet anyway. Obi was so caught up in her daydream she totally lost track of time as well as what was happening in the classroom.

Suddenly, to her surprise, Obi heard the school

bell ring. Then she heard kids excitedly jump up from their desks. She heard Mrs. Creesy hastily assign a homework assignment. Obi, who had no idea what was going on, was dying to peek out of the white canopy, but she didn't dare—she was too worried one of the students walking near the classroom window might spy her little head poking out. Before long, the classroom became very quiet. Finally, Obi decided it was safe for her to peer out from the back of the covered wagon.

The entire classroom was empty. Even Mrs. Creesy was gone. Obi's gaze fell upon Mrs. Creesy's desk. The blue folder was still there, still lying on her desk!

Obi was all alone in an empty classroom with the blue folder that had Rachel's homework assignment sitting on Mrs. Creesy's desk! The temptation was too great for Obi to resist. She crept out of the covered wagon and stole across the window ledge to Mrs. Creesy's desk. She took a running leap and jumped onto it. Then she hurried over to the blue folder, and using both front paws, she lifted the front cover.

The folder was thick with homework papers. Obi began shuffling through them, searching for Rachel's paper. She found it stuck in the middle of the pile.

Obi hesitated. At long last, she was about to find out who Rachel had written about, who she had said was her favorite pet.

Just as Obi was about to start reading, though, something outside the classroom window caught her eye. Something big and yellow. Obi glanced over. It was a school bus. A number of school buses were lined up in the turnaround area that was in front of the school. Students were boarding them. One of the students was Rachel! She, Grace, and Liam all had their school backpacks slung over their shoulders as they stood lined up waiting to climb onto a school bus!

Stunned, Obi glanced over at Rachel's cubby. It was empty! All the cubbies were empty! All the backpacks—including Rachel's blue backpack—were gone!

Rachel was going home!

Terrified that she was about to be left at school, Obi leaped off the edge of Mrs. Creesy's desk. She hit the linoleum-tiled floor, running! She scurried across the classroom and dashed out into the school hallway. There, just outside of Mrs. Creesy's classroom, Obi froze.

Mrs. Creesy stood in the hallway, just a few feet from her classroom doorway, with her arms folded, talking to a mother. There was no way Obi could get past them without one of them spotting her.

Obi spun about and dashed back into the classroom. She climbed up onto Mrs. Creesy's desk and, without hesitating, jumped onto the window ledge. Obi raced over to the large, papier-mâché volcano that sat on the window ledge. She scrambled up the volcano cone, past a stream of painted red lava flow. It was a steep climb! When Obi got to the top of the volcano, she stood up on her hind legs. Standing on the narrow brim of the mouth of the volcano, Obi faced the classroom window.

"MOM! MOM!" Obi cried out, frantically waving her front paws in the air, hoping to catch Rachel's attention.

"MOM, LOOK OVER HERE! LOOK OVER AT MRS. CREESY'S CLASSROOM WINDOW! IT'S ME! OBI! YOU

CAN'T GO HOME! YOU CAN'T! NOT YET! NOT WITHOUT ME!"

In heartbreaking dismay, Obi watched as Rachel stepped into the school bus. The door to the school bus folded closed! That was when Obi went berserk! She began jumping up and down on the edge of the crater, waving her front paws wildly about in the air, doing everything she could think of to try and catch Rachel's eye. She could see Rachel in one of the school bus windows—she had sat down next to Grace; Liam was in the seat in front of them, turned around, talking to them. The school bus started to take off!

"MOM! WAIT! STOP!" Obi shouted.

Suddenly, as she was hysterically leaping up and down, Obi lost her footing! Her heart skipped a beat as she began to fall backward, into the crater!

"WHOA!" she yelled out.

To keep from falling, Obi tried to grab hold of something—*anything*! But there was nothing to grab hold of! Just the mouth of the crater that was painted red to look murderously hot! Obi tumbled down into the dark main vent of the volcano. Down, down, down she dropped! Finally, she landed, hard, on her bum-bum. She was all alone, trapped in the hollow pit of the magma chamber that was in the center of the volcano—all alone and surrounded by darkness.

And the worst part was, nobody knew she was there!

Chapter Twelve The Volcano

Whenever things got really
desperate for Obi, she always tried to keep a positive
attitude, to look on the bright side of things. That was
just her sunny nature. But as far as Obi could tell,
there really wasn't a whole lot to be positive about
at that moment. Here she was stuck in the pit of a
volcano, all alone, and nobody knew it! Not only that,
but Rachel had gone home from school without her!
Plus, Obi's bum-bum really hurt from landing so hard
when she fell. Things sure looked pretty bleak! Well,
at least Obi had one thing to be glad about: at least
this wasn't a real volcano, with scalding hot molten
lava in the magma chamber!

For the next ten minutes or so, Obi tried to escape from the volcano. With a very determined look
on her face, she scrambled up the main vent of the

volcano. But the vent was covered with a thick coat of red poster paint, which made it very slippery. Obi just couldn't get a good grip. Plus, being made of papier-mâché, the sides of the vent crumbled when Obi stuck her claws into it. She'd climb so far up, lose her hold, then tumble back down to the bottom. It was so frustrating! Not to mention extremely painful to her bum-bum!

Obi refused to give up, though. She kept trying and trying to escape. She was about to give it one more try when, just then, she heard footsteps in the classroom. Obi recognized the footsteps. She had heard them all day long, walking about the classroom.

They were Mrs. Creesy's footsteps!

"HELP! HELP!" cried Obi as she sprang up onto her hind legs. She no longer cared if Mrs. Creesy heard her. In fact, she *wanted* Mrs. Creesy to hear her—she *needed* her to hear her in order to be rescued!

Obi heard the footsteps grow louder as they crossed the floor, getting closer to where the volcano was, where Obi was trapped! Obi's heartbeat quickened. She tilted her head back and peered up into the vent. It was like looking up inside a chimney and seeing a little round hole of daylight way up high. She could see the classroom ceiling. Well, a small glimpse of it, at any rate.

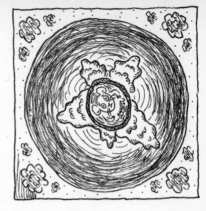

"HELP! HELP! MRS. CREESY! I'M DOWN HERE! I'M DOWN IN THE VOLCANO!"

Obi expected to see Mrs. Creesy's face appear up at the top of the volcano hole, curious to find out who was making all those squeaking noises. But her face didn't appear. Obi, baffled, couldn't understand why not. Then Obi heard what sounded like window blinds being lowered. The light coming down from the vent dimmed. What was going on? Then, to Obi's dismay, she heard Mrs. Creesy walk away from the window! The sound of her footsteps grew fainter. Suddenly, dishearteningly, the overhead lights snapped off and then, all at once, it became very quiet in the classroom.

Mrs. Creesy was gone!

Obi tried not to despair. It wasn't easy. An hour passed. Or was it two hours? Obi had no idea. For all she knew, it might even have been *three* hours! Obi watched as the daylight up at the top of the volcano hole grew dimmer and dimmer as the day turned to night. And then, just when Obi had resigned herself that she was going to have to spend the entire night in the volcano, the classroom lights popped back on! Obi excitedly leaped to her feet.

"HELP! HELP! I'M IN THE VOLCANO! PLEASE, WHOEVER YOU ARE, COME RESCUE ME!"

Obi listened, hoping to hear whoever it was in the classroom rush over to her rescue. But, alas, that did not happen. Obi heard the sound of a wastebasket being emptied. Then she heard a broom being pushed about the floor. Whoever it was had merely come into the classroom to clean. After a few minutes, the person left, turning off the classroom lights.

Once again, Obi found herself in total darkness. She felt more desolate and alone than ever. More time passed. Obi was getting hungry. She heard her stomach growl. She felt so horribly lonely. She missed being in her cage. She missed Rachel. She missed Kenobi. She even missed Wan—well, just a little. The one creature she did not miss, though, was Mr. Durkins.

She was still furious with him! This was all *his* fault!

Obi wondered if Rachel had made the discovery yet that her pet gerbil was gone from her cage. As she sat there in the pitch-black magma chamber, Obi could hear the *tick, tick, tick, tick* of the classroom wall clock. Well, that and her growling stomach. Obi remembered the wonderful aroma of the melted cheese she had smelled earlier that day in the school cafeteria. This, in turn, caused Obi to remember Liam and how shocked he was to see her in the cafeteria and how even more shocked he was to see her in the boys' bathroom and how quickly he had fled the bathroom and how fast she, too, had exited the bathroom and raced down the hallway and into the wrong class—

Obi suddenly remembered something!

The guinea pig!

When she wandered into the wrong classroom, she met that guinea pig! He was in the next classroom! He was probably in his cage right now, right this minute! The thought of the guinea pig being in the next classroom gave Obi hope. But then Obi remembered she was trapped in a darn volcano, and sighed.

But then Obi remembered something else.

Something about herself. She was *Obi, Jedi Gerbil!*
She didn't give up *that* easy!

With a newfound look of fierce determination on her
face, Obi stood on her hind legs. She started to climb
up the volcano vent. This time, though, she tried a
different tact. Instead of racing up the volcano vent
as fast as she could, she took it slowly, methodically,
strategically. First she planted one foot onto the side
of the volcano vent, then another. Slowly, slowly, Obi
made her way up the main vent. Higher and higher,
she climbed. Before long, she reached the top of the
hole. She pulled herself up out of the volcano vent.

Obi was free!

"Woo-hoo!" Obi cried out in
joy. She pumped her fist in the
air in triumph. This caused
Obi to almost lose her balance
and tumble back into the volcano, but, luckily, the gerbil
regained her balance just in time.

Thanks to an outdoor floodlight just outside of Mrs.
Creesy's classroom window, the classroom wasn't as
dark as it might've been. The desks made shadowy

shapes in the dim light. Obi slid down the steep slope of the volcano on her bum-bum. Reaching the bottom, Obi sprang to her feet and raced across the window ledge. As she leaped down to the floor, Obi glanced over at Mrs. Creesy's desk. The blue homework folder was no longer there.

Obi hurried out of the classroom and into the next classroom. It was darker in this classroom—darker and creepier. Obi slowed up as she approached the little table where the guinea pig's cage sat.

"Hawo?" she said tentatively, gazing up to the top of the table. The cage looked like a shadowy smudge in the darkness. "Mr. Guinea Pig? Are you there? It's me . . . Obi. You remember me, don't you? We met today. Remember? I'm the gerbil you scolded because I wasn't where I was supposed to be. You said I'd blow it for everyone. By the way, what did you mean by that?"

Obi paused and listened. She didn't hear a sound. This was not a good sign. She ventured closer to the little table. Obi stopped, rose on her hind legs, and peered up. She had to really strain her eyes to see in the darkness. Her mouth fell open.

The door to the front of the cage was flung open! The guinea pig's cage was empty!

Obi thought she would cry. Even the guinea pig had gone home!

"Oh, my gosh!" wailed Obi. "I'm the only living creature in this whole school tonight!"

Scared and feeling terribly lonely, Obi went back out into the hallway. Being in school all by herself at this hour of night had to be the creepiest place on earth!

Obi began to sob as she wandered aimlessly down the dimly lit school hallway. She was passing the door to the gymnasium when, to her astonishment, she thought she heard noises on the other side of the door. Obi stopped to listen. It sounded like . . . well, like a gym class! But how could that be? It was night, and school was closed for the day! Obi stepped over and put her ear close to the door. Sure enough, she heard voices inside the gymnasium! In a rush of excitement, Obi squeezed under the door.

Never in Obi's wildest dreams did she expect to find what she found on the other side of the gymnasium door. To be honest, she really didn't know what she was expecting to find, but it sure wasn't this!

The lights were on in the enormous, high-ceilinged gymnasium. In the middle of the gymnasium floor was a small group of animals on a blue exercise mat. There was a little hamster, a box turtle, a black bunny, a white bunny, a frog, plus that guinea pig, the one Obi had met earlier that day, the one whose cage was in the classroom next to Mrs. Creesy's classroom. With the exception of the guinea pig, the animals were all jogging around in a circle on the blue exercise mat.

The guinea pig seemed to be the one in charge. He

was shouting at the other animals, telling them that they weren't running fast enough. "C'mon, c'mon! Pick it up! Pick it up!" he kept telling them. "You run like my old grandmother!"

At one point, the guinea pig caught sight of Obi standing by the door, watching. Obi smiled and gave the guinea pig a little wave of her front paw. The guinea pig did not smile or wave back. No, in fact, he glowered at Obi.

"You're late!" he scolded her. "Get over here and give me ten for not showing up on time!"

Obi had no idea what the guinea pig was talking about. Ten? Ten what? And what, for crying out loud, was she late for?

"Ten what?" asked Obi innocently, looking very puzzled as she approached the guinea pig and the other animals who were jogging about on the exercise mat.

The guinea pig stared at her. He had such a hard, penetrating look in his eyes, he scared Obi. Obviously, he was not pleased with her answer.

"Oh, we have an attitude, do we?" he said. "Well, for that, Gerbil, give me twenty!"

Obi frowned. She really had
no clue what the guinea pig
was talking about. "Twenty
what?" she asked.

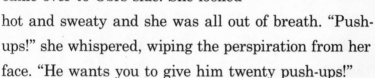

The little hamster slipped
out of the running circle and
came over to Obi's side. She looked
hot and sweaty and she was all out of breath. "Push-
ups!" she whispered, wiping the perspiration from her
face. "He wants you to give him twenty push-ups!"

Obi frowned at the hamster. "Push-ups? What's a
push-up?"

Now it was the hamster who frowned at Obi. "You
don't know what a push-up is?"

Obi shook her head. "No, I don't!"

"Well, don't let Coach know that!" whispered the
hamster. The hamster shot a glance over at the guinea
pig, which made Obi realize that he must be Coach.

"What should I do?" asked Obi worriedly.

"Get down on your stomach and lift yourself up and
down with your paws," the hamster said.

"Do we have a problem here?" the guinea pig suddenly said, fixing his stern gaze on the little hamster. "Why aren't you running?"

"Sorry, Coach!" said the hamster. She gave Obi a quick look and then hurried back into the circle of jogging animals.

The guinea pig now focused his gaze on Obi. "Where are my twenty push-ups?" he demanded.

"Oh! Sorry, Coach!" said Obi. "Here you go!"

Obi dropped down to the floor and did what she thought was a push-up.

The guinea pig was unimpressed. "You call *that* a push-up?" he said, frowning, as he stood over Obi. As Obi did more push-ups, she tried to do them better. "That's the lamest bunch of push-ups I've ever seen!" the guinea pig said. "What's your name again?"

"Obi!"

"Obi, you need to work on your push-ups!"

The guinea pig stepped onto the blue exercise mat to address the other animals. "All right, everyone, listen up!" he said, clapping his two front paws. The animals stopped jogging and peered at the guinea pig. They all looked hot and exhausted. Obi, too, stopped trying to do push-ups. The guinea pig continued, "Tonight we're going to do the rope climb."

Hearing this, a number of the animals groaned. Gesturing to the three ropes that looped down from the gymnasium ceiling, the guinea pig said, "I want each of you to partner up. While one of you climbs, the other will spot. You'll then switch off and the other animal will climb. Any questions?" The guinea pig's eyes flitted from one animal to the next.

Evidently, nobody had any questions.

Well, nobody, that is, but Obi. She raised her front paw.

The guinea pig stared at Obi. He looked surprised. Apparently, he wasn't expecting anyone to ask any questions. "Yes?"

"Does this include me?"

"Uh, you are in this gym class, aren't you?" asked Coach.

Obi thought about this for a moment. She guessed she was. She was here in the gym, after all. "Yes, I guess I am!" she said with a smile.

"What are you smiling about?"

Obi stopped smiling. "Nothing!"

"Well, then, yes, Obi, I guess it does include you!"

"How high are we supposed to climb?"

The guinea pig looked at Obi and said, "How high would you like to climb?"

Obi did not like the way the guinea pig spoke to her. He spoke in a very condescending manner. Obi shrugged and said, "I don't know."

"Well, Obi, you can go as high as you want. Is that okay with you?"

Obi nodded.

"Good then!" said the guinea pig. He glanced about at the other animals, clapping his front paws. "All right, everyone, chop-chop! Find a partner!"

While the guinea pig went to drop the ropes down from the ceiling (which was no easy feat, as he had to leap way up high just to reach the ropes), the little hamster came over to Obi and said, "Want to be my partner?"

"Sure," said Obi.

The hamster smiled. "My name is Sadie."

"Hawo, Sadie! I'm Obi!"

"Do you mind if I go first?" asked Sadie. "I hate the rope climb, and I just want to get it over with."

"Sure, no problem," replied Obi.

"So you'll spot me?"

"Sure. How do I do that?"

"Just keep an eye on me in case I fall. Don't worry, I won't—I don't climb very high. None of us do."

And so, as Sadie climbed up a rope, Obi held the bottom of the rope taut. Sadie didn't get very high— maybe a foot at most—and then she slid back down to the floor. That was about as high as any of the animals climbed. The box turtle didn't even climb *that* high. He grabbed the rope in his mouth, then let go. Apparently, that was what he called climbing a rope.

"Next group!" bellowed the guinea pig.

Obi stood on her hind legs, jumped up, and grabbed hold of the rope with her two front paws. Although she had never climbed up a rope before, Obi felt very confident in her rope-climbing skills. After all, whenever she escaped from her cage, she had to climb the lamp cord that dangled off the side of Rachel's dresser. And just that morning, she had climbed up the cord to Mrs. Creesy's electric pencil sharpener. Plus, Obi was in fantastic shape, from all those endless hours of running on her exercise wheel. So Obi was definitely ready for this.

While Sadie spotted her, Obi began to climb. Of all the animals who were now climbing ropes, Obi was, without a doubt, the fastest rope climber.

"Go, Obi, go!" Obi heard Sadie rooting her on.

This made Obi climb the rope even faster. Out of

the corner of her eye, Obi saw the other animals who were on ropes stop climbing and start to slide down. But Obi wasn't about to stop and slide down. Not yet! She was curious to see just how high she could go. She wanted to climb as high as possible. She wasn't trying to show off. Well, maybe a little. She wanted to show that guinea pig—Coach—a thing or two! She didn't like him making fun of her push-ups. She wanted to show him that, while maybe she couldn't do a push-up to save her life, she was an expert rope climber!

Obi climbed higher and higher. When she was about halfway up from the floor, Obi stopped being an ordinary gerbil. Now, in Obi's mind, she was *Obi, Jedi Gerbil*! Nothing could stop *her* from climbing all the way to the top of the rope and touching the gymnasium ceiling!

And nothing did! In a matter of seconds, Obi reached the top of the rope. She was so pleased and proud of herself! She expected to hear loud cheering from Sadie and all the other animals down on the floor below. She had climbed higher than any of them had climbed!

This was big, big stuff! She was sure they were every bit as pleased and proud of her as she was of herself.

To Obi's baffled surprise, though, she didn't hear any cheering! No! None whatsoever! She didn't even hear any voices! All she heard was silence! She couldn't understand it!

Bewildered, curious, Obi peered down to the floor. She had no idea she had climbed so high! All the animals looked quite small from this high up. They were standing on the blue exercise mat with their heads tilted back and their mouths open in amazement. They were all staring up at Obi with startled, wide-eyed looks.

Obi could not understand this. She had expected them to be delighted and impressed. Why weren't they jumping up and down with excitement at what Obi had accomplished? Even the guinea pig was staring up at her agog.

Obi sighed and began to slide down the rope. When she reached the bottom of the rope, all the animals stood back so she could step off onto the blue mat. As soon as she did, they circled around her, trapping her. They stared at her with the most menacing looks on their faces. Even Sadie, who Obi thought was her friend, had a harsh look in her eyes.

The guinea pig stepped in front of Obi. He got right in her face and said, "Okay, Gerbil, out with it! Who *are* you?"

Chapter Fourteen

The Principal's Spy

"**W**ho am I?" said
Obi, startled, staring
at the guinea pig. She
felt her heart pounding fast. And it wasn't from having just climbed the rope, either. She glanced from
one animal's face to the next. All six animals—the
guinea pig, the little hamster, the white bunny,
the black bunny, the frog, the box turtle—were giving
her the most hostile looks. "I'm . . . I'm Obi!"

"You're a *spy*!" spat the frog.

"*What!?*" cried Obi, taken aback. Incredulous, she
stared at the frog.

"You're a dirty, rotten spy for the principal!" declared the white bunny.

"What are you talking about?" asked Obi, looking
at the white bunny.

"How is it that you're able to climb a rope so well?" demanded the box turtle. "How is it that you're able to climb it better than any of us?"

"Well, for one thing, I don't have a shell like you do," replied Obi. "I'm a bit more agile. Plus, I have an exercise wheel that I run on every day, so I'm in really good shape."

"Oh, so you're saying we're all out of shape?" said Coach. He sounded all huffy and insulted.

"No! I didn't mean it that way!" said Obi quickly. "I'm just saying I guess I'm good at climbing a rope!"

"Or maybe it's because you went to *spy* school!" said Sadie.

"Spy school?" said Obi. "What's *that*?"

"Where spies like *you* go to school and learn to climb ropes and spy on other animals!" said the white bunny.

"I've done no such thing!" exclaimed Obi.

"So you're not a spy for the principal?" asked the black bunny.

"No! Of course not! I'm Rachel's pet!"

"Rachel? Who's Rachel?" asked Sadie.

"She's my owner. She's in Mrs. Creesy's fourth-grade class."

"This is such a bunch of baloney!" cried the frog. "She's a spy for the principal!"

"Why would the principal need a spy?" asked Obi, who really had no idea.

"To find out what we animals do at night!" replied Coach.

"Yeah, and to find out how it is that we're able to escape from our cages!" said the box turtle.

"How do you escape?" asked Obi, who suddenly was very curious to find out. She knew how *she* snuck out of her cage, and she was keenly interested to hear how they got out of theirs. It was a sharing trade secrets sort of thing.

"Ha! So you *are* the principal's spy!" declared the frog. "Why else would you want to know?"

"I'm just curious, that's all!" explained Obi.

"C'mon, admit it, baby!" said the frog. "You were sent here by the principal!"

"I was not!"

"Then prove it!" said the black bunny.

"Yeah, take the I'm-Really-Not-the-Principal's-Spy Test!" cried the white bunny.

"I'd be happy to!" replied Obi. "Just tell me what I need to do!"

But, apparently, none of the animals had any idea of what Obi needed to do to take the test. To discuss the matter, they formed a huddle. Obi watched as the six animals, all bunched together, talked in low voices and occasionally glanced suspiciously over at Obi. Finally, the animals broke out of their huddle and came back over to Obi.

"All right," said the frog, "here's how you can prove that you're not a spy for the principal. You have to steal something from her office."

Obi stared at the frog. She was horrified. Was he serious? "Are you serious?" she cried. But she could tell from the stern look on his face that, yes, he was serious—dead serious. She peered at the other animals. They looked every bit as serious as the frog. They were all staring at Obi.

"You want me to *steal* something from the principal's office?"

"That's how we'll find out if you're her spy or not," explained Sadie. "If you have a close working relationship with the principal, there's no way you'll steal something from her."

"But I can't steal from the principal!" protested Obi.

"Ha! See that?" said the frog, shooting a look at the other animals. "She *is* a spy for the principal! She has qualms about stealing from her!"

"Yes, as a matter of fact, I do!" admitted Obi. "But it's not because I'm a spy! I'm just not the kind of gerbil who likes to steal things!"

"Well, if you want to prove you're not her spy," said the white bunny, "you're going to need to pass the I'm-Really-Not-the-Principal's-Spy Test!"

Obi saw she really had no choice. She had to prove to them she wasn't a spy for the principal. "Okay, okay!" she said. "I'll steal something! But just for the record, I'm doing it against my better judgment!"

Before leaving the gymnasium, Coach quickly ran around the enormous room, pulling up the climbing ropes, moving the exercise mat (all by himself, too!), turning off the overhead lights. He was such an amazing athlete—jumping, climbing, pushing, pulling! Obi was awestruck as she watched the guinea pig race about at a dizzying speed to put everything back just the way it was so nobody would have a clue that a guinea pig, a frog, a hamster, a box turtle, two bunnies, and Obi had been there, working out.

Obi followed the animals out of the gymnasium. As they all made their way down the hallway to the principal's office, the black bunny waddled up beside Obi. "Have we met before?" she asked.

"I don't believe so," replied Obi.

"You look so familiar to me," said the black bunny. "I wonder why?"

"I have no idea," said Obi.

The animals wandered down one hallway, then down another. Eventually they came to a door that was closed. But Coach, by leaping up and grabbing hold of the doorknob and twisting it, was able to open it.

"Okay, here we are at the principal's office!" said Coach.

All of the animals, including Obi, stopped and peered curiously into the principal's office. Although the office was empty, being the principal's office, there was something very intimidating about the place. It was a large office with framed pictures on the walls.

From the doorway, Obi saw a walnut bookcase filled with books; two tall, drab-gray metal file cabinets; twin companion office armchairs in front of a big oak desk; and a desk computer that sat on a side table beside the big oak desk.

"So what do I need to steal?" asked Obi. She certainly hoped it wasn't going to be a file cabinet or the computer or something heavy like that. How would she ever manage to steal such a thing?

"Go up onto the desk and then we'll tell you what to take," said the box turtle.

Obi gave a sigh and went over to the electrical cord to the computer. She climbed up it to the table where the computer was. From there, Obi crossed over to the principal's desk.

"Okay, I'm on top of the desk," Obi reported to the other animals down on the floor. Their heads were tilted back as they peered up at Obi. "What should I take?"

"What's up there?" asked the white bunny.

"Well, I see pictures of some little kids—they must be the principal's kids. And I see a pencil and a pen and some papers and . . ."

Obi's voice trailed off. Her eye had fallen upon a white sheet of paper with typing on it that was all by itself on the desk blotter—like it had been placed there at the end of the day. Being able to read, Obi had no problem reading what it said. It was a print-out of an e-mail announcement that the principal had sent to parents of students that afternoon. The e-mail was marked "Importance: High!"

Your child may tell you tonight that a few students spotted a rat in school today. I want you to know we have thoroughly investigated the matter and have determined that the school does **NOT** have a rat problem! We can only conclude that the students must have imagined they saw a rat. Nonetheless, we will continue to monitor the situa—

"Did you find something?" Obi heard Sadie ask.

"What?" said Obi, who was so focused on reading the principal's e-mail she hadn't heard Sadie's question.

"Did you find something?"

"Uh . . . no, nothing!" replied Obi quickly, stepping away from the e-mail announcement. She didn't want to tell the animals that the principal had sent out an e-mail to all the parents that some students thought they had seen a rat in school today. Particularly since that "rat" had been Obi! She had no idea how the other animals would react to such news, and she wasn't about to find out.

"So what else is up there?" asked the frog.

Obi noticed a small, blue, spongy-looking ball. It had the words STRESS BALL printed on it.

"She has a stress ball," Obi reported.

"What's a stress ball?" asked Coach.

"Oh, my teacher has one!" said the black bunny. "She uses it whenever her students get out of hand. She squeezes the stress ball and it calms her rattled nerves."

"Steal that!" cried the box turtle. "Steal the stress ball!"

"STEAL THE STRESS BALL! STEAL THE STRESS BALL!" the rest of the animals began to chant. "STEAL THE STRESS BALL!"

"What should I do with it?" asked Obi as she picked

up the sponge ball. She was
surprised by how feathery
light it was. Still, even
though it was very light,
Obi hoped the animals weren't

going to make her carry the stress ball around with
her all night.

Obi's question led to another mini-conference
among the animals. From up on top the principal's
desk, Obi patiently waited as the animals on the floor
huddled together to discuss what Obi should do with
the stress ball.

At last, the group broke out of their huddle and the
black bunny said, "Hide it behind her computer!"

Using her two front paws, Obi rolled the small
sponge ball around to the back of the desk computer.
She hid the ball so the principal wouldn't be able to
see it from her desk chair. As Obi pushed it right up
close to the back of the computer, she gave the stress
ball a couple of squeezes. It felt good to squeeze! It felt
very calming!

"Done!" Obi announced as she came around from
behind the computer. To her surprise, Obi found she

got a thrill out of hiding the stress ball, out of being naughty. In fact, she was so excited by what she had done, she wasn't watching where she was stepping. Her left rear foot accidentally touched some of the keys on the computer keyboard. This caused the computer screen to instantly light up.

"What did you do up there?" cried the white bunny in alarm.

"I'm—I'm not sure!" replied Obi worriedly as her eyes nervously flicked back and forth between the computer keyboard and the computer screen. The computer screen showed a list of five names. They were the names of the students whose birthdays were tomorrow. Obi knew this because at the top of the list it said "Tomorrow's Birthdays!" Obi remembered how the principal had gone on the school PA system that morning and read the names of students whose birthdays had been that day. These must be the names of tomorrow's birthday students that she intended to read over the PA system in the morning.

"What did you do to the computer?" asked the frog.

"My foot accidentally touched some of the keys on the computer keyboard."

"You should be more careful!" cried Coach.

Obi was studying the list of names. It looked like she had erased a couple of letters from each student's name. "I think I can fix what I did!" Obi told the animals. With her two front paws, Obi went to correct what she had done. But her two front paws were not accustomed to typing on a computer keyboard. She was clumsy. Instead of adding letters, she deleted letters. This caused her to become flustered, more clumsy! Then, when she went to repair the new damage she had caused, she added too many letters!

"Darn it all!" Obi cried, annoyed at herself for making things even worse.

"What's going on up there?" Coach demanded. Was Obi imagining it or did Coach sound nervous? He didn't seem like the nervous type.

"Nothing!" replied Obi.

Being very careful this time, Obi fixed the names that were on the principal's birthday list. At least she fixed them the best she could. The problem was, as Obi discovered as she typed, computer keyboards are not made for little gerbil paws.

"All fixed!" cried Obi.

"Good!" said the box turtle. "Now, c'mon down from there and let's get out of here!"

Obi leaped off the desk. She landed on the carpeted floor in front of the other animals. They all broke out into nervous giggles as they hurried out in the hallway. Even Obi laughed. She wasn't the kind of gerbil who would ever think of hiding a principal's stress ball, but, honestly, it was fun being a little naughty. Not that she intended to make a habit of it, but every once in while, she thought, why not?

The best part was, Obi was no longer suspected of being the principal's spy. She had passed the I'm-Really-Not-the-Principal's-Spy Test. Indeed, she had passed it with flying colors! She had been accepted by the other animals.

She was now one of them!

Chapter Fifteen

Teachers' Pets

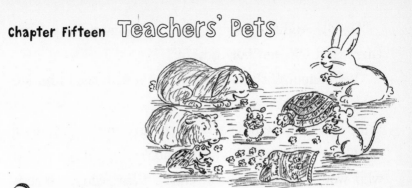

$\textbf{O}$ut in the hallway, the box turtle said, "So what do you guys want to do now?"

Sadie said, "I think we should let Obi decide that."

"I agree!" said the black bunny. "Anyone who passes the I'm-Really-Not-the-Principal's-Spy Test gets to choose what we do next."

Sadie turned to Obi. "So what do you want to do, Obi?"

"Well," said Obi. "I don't know about you guys, but *I'm* starving! I haven't eaten in hours! I wouldn't mind getting something to eat."

"What are you in the mood for?" asked Coach.

"Anything, really. Seeds. Nuts. Grains."

"How do you feel about someone's forgotten lunch?" asked Coach.

Obi thought about it for a moment and then shrugged. "Sure. Why not?"

"Well, then, let's go to the Lost and Found and see what's there," said Coach. "Someone is always forgetting their lunch box on the playground and then it winds up in the Lost and Found."

"Yeah," said the white bunny. "Yesterday someone left a half-eaten cupcake!"

With Coach leading the way, the animals headed down the dimly lit school hallway in the direction of the cafeteria, where, apparently, the Lost and Found room was located. As they walked, the black bunny kept glancing over at Obi. She squinted her eyes at the gerbil, with a troubled look on her face, like something was really bothering her.

"Gosh, you look *so* familiar!" she exclaimed. "I wish I could remember where I've seen you! Are you *sure* we haven't met before?"

"Pretty sure," replied Obi.

Before long they came to a small alcove by the cafeteria. There was a table in the little room; a box was on top of the table. Taped to the front of the box was a sheet of white paper that had big, colorful letters in all different fonts printed on it.

LOST & FOUND!!!

The animals stopped on the floor before the table and peered up at the cardboard box. "We're in luck!" cried Coach. "See that cardboard box, Obi? That box holds all sorts of things that students have lost in or around school—baseball caps, water bottles, little rubber balls, gloves, mittens, pens, hair scrunchies, you name it. But what we're interested in, Obi, is *that!*" The guinea pig pointed a front paw at a metal lunch box that sat on the table, right beside the cardboard box. The front of the lunch box had a colorful picture of Harry Potter, Ron Weasley, and Hermione Granger on it. "Inside that lunch box is someone's leftover lunch!"

While Obi and the other animals watched, Coach shimmied up one of the table legs. He pulled himself up onto the table and hurried over to the Harry Potter lunch box. Obi watched in awe as Coach, using his two front paws, set the lunch box down on its side. With a little jiggering of the latch, Coach popped open the top of the lunch box.

Coach immediately sprang back from the opened lunch box. *"Stink bomb!"* he wailed, his face all scrunched up in disgust. "Leftover liverwurst sandwich gone bad!"

Holding a paw over his nose and moving quickly, Coach stepped toward the lunch box. He reached in, and pulled out an unopened snack-size bag of popcorn. He tossed the small bag of popcorn down to the floor, then he himself jumped off the table. He landed in front of the animals.

Obi was very impressed by the Coach's athletic skills. No wonder the guinea pig was called "Coach!"

Coach tore open the small bag of popcorn and held it out to Obi.

Obi was touched that Coach offered her the popcorn first. She was wrong about Coach, she could see that now. Despite her first impressions of him being something of a big, bossy loudmouth, he was really a very nice guinea pig. "Thanks so much, Coach!" said Obi as she helped herself to a piece of popcorn. Then Coach offered the bag to the other animals. "Popcorn, anyone?" he said.

"So, Obi," said the white bunny as the animals all sat together on the cafeteria floor, munching away on what turned out to be cheddar-flavored popcorn, "if you don't go to school here, where do you go to school?"

"I don't go to any school," replied Obi.

"Oh, so you're homeschooled?" said Sadie.

Obi shrugged. She really didn't know if she was or not. "I guess so."

"I don't really get homeschool," said the black bunny, making a face, as she glanced around at the other animals. "If I was home all day, I'd sure miss all you guys."

"And we'd sure miss you!" said the white bunny.

"Oh, sorry, Obi, I didn't mean to offend you," said the black bunny. "You know, about what I said about homeschooling."

"No offense taken," replied Obi.

"And, Obi, you say you're the pet of someone named Rachel?" asked Coach.

"Yes," replied Obi, nodding. "Rachel Armstrong. She's in Mrs. Creesy's fourth-grade class."

"So you're *not* a teacher's pet?" asked the box turtle.

Obi shook her head. "No," she replied. "Why? Are you?"

"We're *all* teachers' pets!" said Sadie.

"I'm Mrs. Fazio's pet!" said the black bunny proudly. "I'm in second grade!"

"And I'm Miss Lloyd's pet!" said the frog. "I'm in first grade!"

"Einstein is a math wiz, you know," said Coach.

Obi frowned. "Einstein? Who's Einstein?" she asked.

"Oh, for heaven's sake!" cried the black bunny. "Where are our manners? We haven't introduced ourselves to Obi!"

"Speak for yourselves!" said Sadie. "I have! Haven't I, Obi?"

Obi was nibbling on a piece of popcorn. She didn't want to speak with her mouth full so she just nodded.

"I'm Einstein!" the frog said to Obi.

Swallowing, Obi said, "Hawo, Einstein!"

"And I'm Coach!" said the guinea pig.

"Hawo, Coach!"

"And I'm Ramona!" said the black bunny. "I'm named after—"

"Ramona Quimby!" said Obi.

The black bunny's eyes widened. She looked shocked. "Why, yes! How did you know?"

"I'm familiar with the books," replied Obi.

"I'm Pablo!" said the white bunny.

"Hawo, Pablo!"

"And I'm Clarence!" said the box turtle.

"Hawo, Clarence!"

"I'm named after Clarence Clemens!"

"Really!" said Obi. "And who is he?"

The box turtle made a face. "I have no idea!"

"Well, it's so nice to meet you all," said Obi. Turning to the frog, Obi said, "So, Einstein, you're a math wiz?"

Looking very bashful, the frog lowered his eyes. "That's what they say," he replied, gesturing at the other animals.

"Oh, don't be so modest!" exclaimed Ramona, the black bunny, in a voice that almost sounded like she was scolding him. "Go ahead, Obi, ask

 him something! Ask him what
two plus two equals."

Obi peered at Einstein and
said, "What does two plus

two equal?"

The frog broke into a big grin and shouted out,
"NINE!"

"Isn't he amazing!?" Ramona said, marveling at the
frog.

"He certainly is!" said Obi. Having never studied
math, Obi had no idea if Einstein's answer was correct or not. But it sounded good.

For his part, Einstein looked pleased as anything
by all the compliments he was receiving.

"Now ask him what five plus five equals!" said
Ramona.

"What does five plus five equal?" Obi asked.

"TWO!"

"What's three plus two?" asked Coach.

"TEN!"

"One plus one?"

"FIFTEEN!"

"Gosh, I wish I knew math as well as you!" said

Pablo, the white bunny. "I'm so envious of your math skills, Einstein!"

The frog shyly looked down at
the floor.

"Clarence, here, is our science ex-
pert," said Sadie, patting the box turtle on the top of
his shell. "Clarence, tell Obi the planets in the solar
system in the order that they appear from the sun."

The box turtle closed his eyes in concentration. Then
his eyes flew open and, in rapid-fire quickness, he sput-
tered out: "Saturn! Pluto! The Hubble
space telescope! Uranus! The
Big Dipper! Jupiter! Earth!
Mercury! Mars! The Little
Dipper! Venus! The international
space station! The North Star! Neptune! Earth's
moon!"

Everyone applauded. Even Obi clapped her two
front paws.

Sadie pointed at the guinea pig. "And Coach's spe-
ciality is—"

"Let me guess," said Obi. "Gymnastics!"

"No, knitting!" said the guinea pig.

Obi frowned. "*Knitting?* Seriously?"

"Just kidding!" cried Coach, and burst out laughing. "Yes, I'm the gymnastics expert!"

"And you, Sadie, what do you do?" asked Obi.

"I work with special needs children. I'm in Miss Rivera's special needs class."

"Gosh, you're all so talented!" said Obi.

"What are you good at, Obi?" asked Clarence, the box turtle.

"Well, I can read a little," replied Obi modestly.

"*Really!*" said Coach, looking very impressed.

"And I can tell stories," said Obi.

"You can tell stories!?" exclaimed Einstein, the frog.

"Tell us a story! Tell us a story!" cried Ramona, the black bunny, gleefully.

Obi was quiet for a moment as she tried to think of a good story to tell. She wanted to tell a story that the animals could relate to, which meant, she felt, telling a story about either a guinea pig, a hamster, a frog, a bunny, or a turtle. Obi couldn't think of any guinea pig stories, or any hamster stories, or even a frog story, although she was sure she knew one.

"How about a bunny story?" asked Ramona. "Know any bunny stories?"

"As a matter of fact, I do!" said Obi. She was about to tell them *The Runaway Bunny* when her gaze fell upon Clarence, the box turtle, and she abruptly changed her mind about telling that story. Instead of telling them a story that was only about a bunny, she would tell a story that was about both a bunny *and* a turtle.

So that was what Obi did. She told them the old Aesop fable about the bunny and the tortoise who were in a race together. Ramona, the black bunny, and Pablo, the white bunny, both smiled with pleasure when Obi got to the part about how speedy-fast the bunny was, and how he left the turtle in the dust at the start of the race. But then Obi got further into the story and told them how the bunny got so far ahead in the race, the bunny became a bit too over-confident in himself and decided to take a little nap, which was a big, big mistake for it allowed the turtle to catch up and beat him in the race.

When Ramona and Pablo heard this, their faces fell.

"And so the moral of the story is," said Obi, "slow and steady wins the race."

"I'm not sure I like this story," said Ramona.

"I'm not sure I do, either," said Pablo.

"I love it!" said Clarence, the box turtle, beaming.

Obi felt awful that she had made Ramona and Pablo feel bad. So she decided to make up another ending to the story. "The good news is," Obi said, "the bunny learned from his mistake. The next race he was in, which was with a cheetah, the fastest animal on earth, he won!"

The bunnies looked absolutely delighted to hear this new ending to the fable. They both burst into big, broad smiles. "Hooray for the bunny!" cried Ramona, clapping her two front paws.

When the bunnies' excitement died down, Sadie

said, "So, Obi, tell us, what are doing here in school?"

"Yes, why are you here?" asked Ramona. "Not that we don't like you being here."

"I'm here to find out who Rachel wrote about in her homework paper," said Obi. She explained to them about how Mrs. Creesy had given her class a homework assignment in which each of the students had to write about their favorite pet. "I wanted to find out who Rachel had written about," continued Obi. "So I snuck into Rachel's backpack to read her paper. I was in her backpack when I heard Rachel zip it up. One thing led to another and the next thing I knew I found myself here in school. And all I wanted to do was find out who Rachel said is her favorite pet."

"And who did she say is her favorite pet?" asked Sadie.

Obi shrugged. "I still haven't found out."

"Well, what do you say we all go find out now?" said Coach.

"Well, we could," said Obi, "but, unfortunately, I don't know where her homework paper is. I saw Mrs. Creesy put all the homework papers in a blue folder, but I have no idea where she put the blue folder."

"Well, it's got to be in her classroom somewhere," said Pablo. "We'll help you look for it."

With that, they all headed down the school hallway in the direction of Mrs. Creesy's classroom. They hadn't gone far when Ramona came to a sudden halt. She stopped in the school hallway, eyes wide, staring at Obi.

"I know where I've seen *you!*" she blurted out.

"Where?" asked Obi as she, too, stopped.

"There!" exclaimed the bunny, and pointed to the hallway wall that was behind Obi.

Chapter Sixteen

The Whoopee Cushion

Turning, Obi saw that Ramona was pointing to a bulletin board that was on the hallway wall, right across from a door that had the words **ART ROOM** printed beside it. The bulletin board was covered with watercolor drawings of animals—dogs, cats, beavers, chimpanzees, an elephant, a rhinoceros, a hippopotamus, and, curiously enough, a gerbil. Obi stared at the gerbil drawing. The gerbil looked stunningly like Obi!

"Will you look at *that*!" marveled Coach in amazement as his eyes glanced from Obi to the drawing of the gerbil on the bulletin board and then back to Obi. "That gerbil in that drawing looks just like you, Obi!"

The drawing did look like her! In fact, it was Obi—Rachel had printed Obi's name up at the top of the drawing and her own name down by the bottom! Obi was so proud of her adoptive mother and thrilled that Rachel's drawing had been selected for the school hallway bulletin board. Obi couldn't get over the fact that a drawing of herself was on display in school! She felt like she was a famous celebrity!

"Rachel, my owner, drew that!" exclaimed Obi.

"She sure is a good drawer!" said Pablo.

"Oh, she's an excellent drawer!" said Obi. "I mean, I know she's my adoptive mom and all, and so, of course, I can't be impartial, but she really is an unbelievably good drawer!"

"I *knew* I'd seen you somewhere!" said Ramona. The bunny looked pleased as anything—as well as somewhat relieved—that she had finally figured out where she had seen Obi.

When the animals had finished admiring Rachel's drawing, they continued on their way down the hallway to Mrs. Creesy's classroom. Entering the classroom, they got right to work searching for the blue folder. They looked everywhere for it. Under the students' desks. On the row of desks where the classroom computers sat. Along the classroom window ledge. In the bookcase by the student cubbies. In the cubbies themselves. They even looked in the metal wastebasket by Mrs. Creesy's desk.

Obi, Sadie, and Ramona searched the top of Mrs. Creesy's desk for the blue folder. At one point, Einstein, the frog, hopped up onto Mrs. Creesy's desk chair. From there, he bounced into a desk drawer that was slightly opened. It was the same desk drawer that Obi had hidden in earlier that day. The frog momentarily disappeared from view. Then, suddenly, a loud fart exploded from inside the drawer.

"Oh, Einstein!" cried Ramona, frowning in disapproval when the frog popped his head back up out of the drawer.

"What?" he asked, with an innocent look on his face.

"You know perfectly well what!" admonished the black bunny. "A polite frog, Einstein, would excuse himself after making such a horrid noise!"

"But that wasn't *me!*"

"Einstein, I heard *you*!" replied Ramona. "I heard *you* loud and clear!"

"But it wasn't *me*!" protested Einstein. "There's something in this drawer that made that sound! I just happened to hop on it!"

"He's right," said Obi, who had been listening to their conversation while searching for the blue folder in a stack of folders that was on Mrs. Creesy's desk. "I had to hide in that same drawer earlier today. There's a rubber pillow in the drawer that makes that sound when you press down on it."

"Oh!" said Ramona. She looked aghast that such a thing existed.

"See!" Einstein said to Ramona. "I told you it wasn't me!"

"It's called a whoopee cushion," said Obi, her eyes moving from Einstein to Ramona and then to Sadie, who had stopped to listen. "Rachel's brother has one— that's how I know what it is."

"Well, it certainly makes the most dreadful sound!" declared Ramona.

"It only makes that sound when it has air in it,"

said Obi. "I guess it must've still had some air in it when Einstein hopped on it."

"I guess so," said Ramona.

"Any luck?" Coach's voice called up from down on the floor.

Obi stepped over to the edge of the desk and peered down. Coach, Clarence, and Pablo were at the bottom of the desk, peering up.

"No, nothing!" reported Obi. "The blue folder isn't on the desk!"

Obi was about to say she thought they should call off the search when, from within Mrs. Creesy's desk drawer, a second loud fart unexpectedly exploded. A moment later, Einstein's head popped up out of the desk drawer. He had a huge grin on his amphibian face. For a laugh, Einstein had gone back into the drawer and, evidently, blown more air into the whoopee cushion and then leaped onto it.

The frog was not disappointed for his efforts. The rude noise caused Coach, Clarence, and Pablo to burst out into hysterical laughter. They could not stop laughing. At one point, Pablo, the white bunny, began rolling around on the linoleum-tiled floor, he was so overcome with the giggles.

Obi, watching, rolled her eyes. Then she, too, laughed. She couldn't resist. She glanced over at Sadie and Ramona and saw that they, too, were laughing.

Finally, Sadie said, "All right, guys, that's enough!" The little hamster turned to Obi and said, "I hate to say it, Obi, but it doesn't look like the blue folder is anywhere in this classroom."

Ramona said, "Mrs. Creesy must've brought the blue folder home. She must've had more homework papers she had to grade."

"I guess," sighed Obi.

"I'm sure you'll find out before too long who Rachel said is her favorite pet," said Sadie. "And when you do, Obi, I'm sure it'll be you!"

Obi smiled. Then, all together at the same time, she, Sadie, and Ramona, jumped down off the desk. They landed on the floor in front of Coach, Pablo, and Clarence.

"Well, guys, thank you for helping me look for the blue folder," Obi said as they crossed the classroom on their way to the doorway. "It means a lot to me that you did that."

"Sorry we were unable to find it," said Clarence.

"Don't give it another thought," said Obi.

"Well, we'd best be getting back to our cages," said Coach. "It's getting late and we need to get a good night's sleep. We all have school tomorrow."

"That's right!" said Ramona. "We do!"

"So what are your plans, Obi?" asked Sadie.

Obi shrugged and said, "I guess I'll hang out in Mrs. Creesy's classroom and just lie low until the end of the school day tomorrow. Then I'll climb back into Rachel's backpack and go home with her."

"Well, since it doesn't sound like I'll be seeing you again, Obi, I guess this is good-bye," said Coach.

This hadn't occurred to Obi. "Yes, I . . . I guess it is," she said. Obi suddenly felt terribly sad.

"Where's Einstein?" Sadie asked, looking all about.

"I don't know!" said Coach as he, too, glanced about the classroom. "He was here just a minute ago."

"Here I am!" cried Einstein, hopping toward them from out of the shadows. He came from the direction of Mrs. Creesy's desk.

"Where did you go?" asked Sadie.

"Nowhere!" said Einstein. As the frog said this, Obi thought she detected a little twinkle in his eyes.

There was no twinkle in Ramona's eyes, however. She looked like she was about to burst into tears. "I'm so sorry, Obi!" she wailed as she gave the gerbil a big hug. "I hate good-byes! Just hate them! They make me so, so sad!" And with that, she spun about and scurried out of the classroom.

Then Coach, Pablo, Clarence, and Einstein each gave Obi a hug. Then they, too, hurried out of the classroom. It surprised Obi how emotional everyone—including herself—was at having to say good-bye. She'd only known these animals for a few hours. Yet, she felt like she'd known them forever. She'd had so much fun with them, that was the thing!

Now only Sadie was left. "Well, good-bye, Obi," she said. "I'll miss you!"

"I'll miss you, too, Sadie," said Obi. "Thanks again for all your help tonight."

"Oh, I didn't do anything!"

"You showed me how to do push-ups," said Obi.

Sadie chuckled. "Yes, I guess I did do that, didn't I? You'll keep in touch, won't you, Obi?"

"I'll try to!" promised Obi. But she knew, just as Sadie must've known, that the chances of them keeping in touch were next to nil. This thought made Obi even sadder.

Tears filled Obi's eyes as she watched Sadie turn and leave the classroom. Just before the little hamster disappeared out into the hallway, she stopped, turned, and gave Obi a little wave of her front paw. As Obi waved back, she saw that Sadie, too, had tears in her eyes.

And then Obi found herself all alone again.

"I guess I'd better get some sleep," she murmured, wiping the tears from her eyes. She glanced about the classroom, wondering where to sleep that night. She thought about bedding down in the Oregon Trail covered wagon, but then her gaze fell upon Rachel's desk and, suddenly, she knew exactly where she would sleep that night. She walked over to Rachel's desk and shimmied up one of the legs—just the way Coach had done when he climbed up onto the Lost and Found table. Obi was sorry Coach wasn't there to see her following his example. He would've been so pleased, she thought.

There was a little cubby space under the writing surface of Rachel's desk. In this little cubby space, Obi discovered Rachel's writing pads, pens and pencils, plus a couple of textbooks. Obi made herself comfortable on top of a yellow lined pad. As she curled up to go to sleep, Obi wondered what Rachel was doing at that moment, back at home. She wondered if Rachel had discovered that Obi was missing from her cage.

Just as Obi was about to close her eyes, she noticed something. She sat up and peered at the yellow lined pad. There were three little doodles on the top sheet. In the feeble light that spilled into the classroom from

the hallway, Obi could just make out each drawing.

One doodle was of a planet that looked like some faraway, dream-like, magical world.

Another doodle was of a tree, an ancient tree with an enormous trunk and lots of branches and leaves.

And the last doodle? It was of a little gerbil who bore an astonishing resemblance to Obi!

All at once, a wave of tremendous exhaustion came over Obi. But with this wave of tremendous exhaustion came a wave of tremendous happiness, too. The little gerbil once again curled up on top of the yellow notepad and closed her eyes.

A moment later, she was fast asleep.

Chapter Seventeen   Rachel's Homework Paper

"**Obi? Obi?** Where are you?"

The voice was that of a little creature. A female creature. The voice sounded urgent, frantic. In her sleep, Obi mumbled something unintelligible. Or at least she thought she did. Being asleep, she really didn't know if she actually said anything or not.

"Obi? Where are you?"

Who could be calling her? Was she dreaming? Obi was too sleepy to answer or open her eyes.

"OBI!? WHERE ARE YOU!?"

Obi woke up with a start. Now fully awake, she peered about her in bewilderment, wondering where she was and who was calling her name. She wasn't in her cage—she was in a strange classroom, in a desk in a classroom. But why? Where? Then, all of a sudden, Obi remembered whose classroom this was and whose desk she was sleeping in and why she was there.

"Where are you, Obi?" cried the voice again.

Obi peered down from her perch in Rachel's desk cubby and saw a little hamster wandering about on the floor, her eyes flicking about, searching for Obi.

"Sadie?"

The little hamster looked up. "Oh! *There* you are!" she cried.

"What are you doing here, Sadie?"

"I'm looking for *you!*"

Obi glanced out the classroom window and saw that it was daylight out. She saw blue sky and puffy white clouds above the school playground. "But it's daytime," said Obi. "Shouldn't you be back in your cage?"

"I should, but I saw Mrs. Creesy and—"

"You *saw* Mrs. Creesy!" cried Obi, her eyes wide with alarm. "Where is she? You can't be seen in her classroom, Sadie! Neither can I!"

"Don't worry!" said Sadie. "She's not here! I'm pretty sure she went to the teachers' lounge! She'll be back soon, though, so we don't have much time!"

"Much time to do what?"

"To find the blue folder!"

"The blue folder? What are you talking about? We couldn't find it last night, remember?"

"Yes, I know but I saw Mrs. Creesy walk past my classroom on her way here. She had on her coat and she was carrying a briefcase. About five minutes later, I saw Mrs. Creesy again outside my classroom, this time heading in the direction of the teachers' lounge. She didn't have her coat on and she wasn't carrying a briefcase. I bet you anything the blue folder is in that briefcase! She might even have taken the blue folder out. It's *got* to be here in this classroom!"

Obi glanced over at Mrs. Creesy's desk. Being in the cubby of Rachel's desk, Obi was up high enough to be able to see the top of Mrs. Creesy's desk.

And there it was—the blue folder—sitting on top of Mrs. Creesy's desk!

"I see it, Sadie!" exclaimed Obi. "It's on her desk!"

"It is? Excellent!" cried Sadie. "Come on down, Obi, so we can find out who Rachel said is her favorite pet!"

Suddenly trembling with excitement, Obi hopped

down to the floor. She landed on all four paws. Together, she and Sadie raced over to Mrs. Creesy's desk. Obi was the first up to the top of Mrs. Creesy's desk. Sadie was right behind her. The two of them scurried over to the blue folder. Obi grabbed the outside edge of the front of the blue folder. She was about to flip it open when she stopped and let go of the blue folder.

Sadie stared at Obi with a very puzzled look on her face. "What is it?" she asked.

"I don't need to find out who Rachel said is her favorite pet."

"You don't?" Sadie sounded surprised.

Obi shook her head. "No, I don't. I just realized something, Sadie."

"What?"

"Well, I just realized that I don't need to know who Rachel said is her favorite pet. I know that she loves me. If she didn't, she wouldn't have made that really nice drawing of me that's hanging up in the school hallway, outside the art room. You know, the one we saw last night. I also found a little doodle Rachel did of me on one of the writing pads in her desk. Rachel wouldn't have done that if she didn't love me, if I didn't mean something to her. She thinks of me even when I'm not around. So, you see, Sadie, it really doesn't matter to me anymore if I'm her favorite pet or not."

Obi expected Sadie to smile and say something like how she completely understood and that she was glad that Obi had figured this out. To Obi's astonishment, though, a look of anger flashed into Sadie's eyes!

"Well!" she exclaimed. "*You* may not need to find out who Rachel's favorite pet is, but *I* do!"

"What do you mean?"

"I mean," said Sadie, "that ever since you told us about this homework assignment, I can't stop thinking about it. I can't stop wondering who Rachel said is her favorite pet! I can't stop wondering if it's you or if it's that little gerbil named Wan or that puppy named Kenobi! It's driving me nuts! I want it to be you, Obi, and I *have* to find out if it *is* you!"

"Oh, that's so sweet of you!" said Obi.

"So if you think I'm going to stand by and watch you not open that blue folder and find out who Rachel said is her favorite pet, well, think again, Obi!"

To show she meant business, Sadie stood up on her

hind legs and crossed her arms and gave Obi a fierce stare.

Obi couldn't help but smile. "Well, when you put it that way," she said, "I guess I *do* have to find out!"

Using her two front paws, Obi flipped open the front of the blue folder. The blue folder contained a stack of about twenty or so homework papers. The papers tended to be written in pencil or pen, and all were titled "My Favorite Pet!" Obi began flipping through the homework assignments, looking for Rachel's. At the top of each paper Mrs. Creesy, using a red marker, had written a letter grade. Mrs. Creesy had given most of the papers Bs. Obi also saw some B minuses and B pluses, and quite a few Cs and C pluses. What Obi did not see, however, were many A's.

About halfway through the stack of homework papers, Obi came upon Rachel's paper. Obi recognized her adoptive mother's unmistakable handwriting the moment she saw it. Plus, Rachel had written her name in the upper left-hand corner of her paper.

"Here it is!" said Obi, since she knew Sadie could not read.

"So?" said Sadie excitedly. "Who does Rachel say is her favorite pet?"

"I don't know," said Obi. "I haven't read it yet!"

"Well, what are you waiting for?" cried Sadie impatiently. "Read it!"

Despite what Obi had said about not caring if she was Rachel's favorite pet or not, she suddenly became very nervous about finding out who, indeed, really was. Taking a deep breath, Obi began to read.

I have three pets, two gerbils and a puppy. My gerbils are named Obi and Wan. My puppy is named Kenobi. I've had Obi the longest. Wan is my newest pet. He can be so annoying sometimes. Like right this very minute, he is gnawing on the bars of his cage. It drives me crazy when he does that! UGH!!! I get so mad at him!! But Obi, whose cage is right next to Wan's, is the most patient and understanding gerbil. He never gets mad at Wan. Never! Obi is so kind and gentle. I could learn a thing or two from Obi. I love all of my pets, but I have to say that my favorite pet is Obi.

Kenobi, my puppy, is learning how to do tricks. He can lift his paw when you ask him to, but he still hasn't quite figured out how to fetch a—

"So? So who is it?" demanded Sadie. "I can't stand the suspense, Obi! Tell me! Tell me! Who does Rachel say is her favorite pet? Is it you? It is you, isn't it! *I* knew it! Oh, Obi, I'm so happy for you! But wait! Your face doesn't look happy! It isn't you, is it? Oh, Obi, I'm so sorry! You poor thing! I'm sure she—"

"It's okay, Sadie, it is me," said Obi. "I'm Rachel's favorite pet."

Sadie's face lit up. "It is *you*!? Oh, that's fantastic,

Obi! I knew it was you! Congratulations!! You rock, Gerbil!"

"Thanks," said Obi.

"I must say, for someone who just found out she's Rachel's favorite pet, you don't seem very happy about it!"

"No, I am," said Obi. She gave a sigh. "It's just that, well . . ." Her voice trailed off.

"It's just that *what*?"

"Well, it's just that Rachel wrote that I'm all these things that I'm really not."

"Like what?"

"Like that I'm kind and patient and understanding about Wan. But I'm not! I'm not the least bit kind or patient or understanding about Wan! In fact, I can't stand that little brat!"

"Well, I'm sure you're more kind and patient and understanding than you give yourself credit for," said Sadie. "Even so, Obi, it must be pretty nice to know once and for all that you're Rachel's favorite pet."

"It is," admitted Obi, and smiled.

"What grade did Mrs. Creesy give Rachel?" asked Sadie.

"An A minus."

"An A minus!? That's a very good grade!"

"Well, it really is a very well-written paper!" said Obi. She turned Rachel's paper over to see how much more Rachel had written on the other side. Obi's gaze fell upon the paper that was under Rachel's paper. It was Cleo's paper. Cleo had typed her paper on a computer and then printed it out. Obi remembered Cleo all too well. She was the girl who had written about her cat, Theo. Obi also remembered how Cleo had told Rachel and Grace that she was positive she was going to get a really bad grade on this homework assignment.

"Say, Sadie, which is better?" asked Obi. "An A minus or an A plus?"

"Oh, an A plus, without question!" replied Sadie. She paused for a moment and, looking very bewildered, said, "Why do you ask?"

"Well, because Cleo got an A plus."

"Cleo? Who's Cleo?"

"She's another girl in Mrs. Creesy's class. She's very smart and she's always getting better grades than Rachel. She's always saying how badly she did on an assignment and then she always gets a really terrific grade. My mom can't stand her!"

"I can see why!" said Sadie. "Well, Obi, we'd better get off this desk before Mrs. Creesy returns."

"Not before I do something," said Obi.

Sadie, who was already on her way over to the edge of Mrs. Creesy's desk, stopped, turned, and stared at Obi. She looked very concerned. "Like what kind of something?"

"Like I think I'm going to change my adoptive mother's grade kind of something!" replied Obi, with a mischievous gleam in her eyes. "I'm going to give her the same grade as Cleo!"

Sadie stared at Obi. The little hamster looked absolutely horrified. "But, Obi, you can't do that!"

"Why can't I?"

"Because you can't!"

"Why not?"

"Because you'll be tampering with a teacher's grade! You can't change a teacher's grade! Even if it is your adoptive mother's homework paper!"

"I don't see the harm in it!" said Obi. "My mom wrote a really good paper!"

"It doesn't matter!" protested Sadie.

"She deserves a better grade!" insisted Obi.

"You can't change her grade, Obi! You just can't!"

"What if I told you that Cleo wrote about a cat?" said Obi. "A cat named Theo! I don't have to remind you, Sadie, that cats are our archenemies! Nothing would please a cat better than to eat a little gerbil or a little hamster!"

"That doesn't matter, Obi!" said Sadie. "Trust me, I don't like cats any better than you do! But you still can't change Rachel's grade!"

"Let me read you what Cleo wrote about her cat, Theo." Before Sadie could say anything, Obi began to read.

"'My cat, Theo, has got to be the cutest, cleverest pet in the entire world. He's such an amazing cat! Do you know what he likes to do? When my bedroom door is closed and he's on the other side of the door, he sticks his paw under the crack at the bottom of my door to try and get my attention. I'll be in my bedroom and I'll see his front paw moving back and forth. I don't know of any other pet that can do something like that!'"

"I can do that!" Sadie blurted out.

Obi continued to read, "'My cat, Theo, also loves

to hunt. He catches little mice and moles and brings them to our front doorstep. He drops them on the front doormat, like they're little gifts that he's leaving for us to find. Isn't he so cute?'"

Obi stopped reading and looked up at Sadie. "Heard enough?" she asked.

But Sadie didn't say anything. Instead, she went over to a ceramic jar filled with pens and pencils that was on Mrs. Creesy's desk. She pulled out a red marker pen. She brought it back and thrust the marker at Obi.

"Here's a red marker!" said Sadie. "Change Rachel's grade!"

Taking the red marker, Obi smiled. She stood up on her rear legs and, gripping the red marker in her two front paws, she changed Rachel's grade. She really didn't have to do too much. She simply added a little red vertical line to the little red horizontal line. She crossed the red vertical line with the red horizontal line. So the A– became an A+.

Obi stepped back to admire her handiwork. "What do you think?" she asked. "Rachel now has an A plus!"

"Nice!" said Sadie, smiling.

Obi was about to return the red marker to the ceramic jar of pens and pencils when, glancing again at Rachel's paper, something about what she had just done didn't sit well with her. She didn't know why, exactly, but the A+ just didn't look right. It seemed to be missing something. Still holding the red marker, Obi came back to Rachel's paper.

"What are you doing now?" asked Sadie.

"You'll see," replied Obi mysteriously.

What Obi did was add another plus. So Rachel's paper now had two pluses after her A. It looked like this: **A++.**

Obi wasn't quite done yet, though. To top it off, she added some exclamation marks. Three, to be exact. By the time Obi put the red marker back into the ceramic jar, Rachel's grade had gone from an A– to an A++!!!

"You're a real kook, you know that, Obi?" said Sadie affectionately as, laughing, she watched Obi close the blue folder.

"Just correcting a terrible injustice," replied Obi.

"Well, Obi, I'm sure going to miss you!" said Sadie.

"Yeah, I'm sure going to miss you, too, Sadie!" said Obi, and gave Sadie a hug.

"Good luck getting home!" Sadie said as she stepped over to the edge of the desk. She turned and looked back at Obi and said, "Congratulations again on being named Rachel's favorite pet!"

Obi gave her a big smile and said, "Thanks."

With that, Sadie leaped down to the linoleum-tiled floor. Then Obi, too, jumped down from Mrs. Creesy's desk. But in Obi's case, she didn't jump down to the floor but onto the window ledge. She raced across the wide ledge and slipped into the back of the Oregon Trail covered wagon. She poked her head out of the rear of the covered wagon just in time to see the end of Sadie's tail vanish out into the school hallway. Less than a minute later, Mrs. Creesy walked into the classroom, holding a mug of coffee in her hand.

Chapter Eighteen

A Most Unusual Morning

Being in school at that early hour, Obi got a first-hand look at what happens on a school day morning. Well, at least in Mrs. Creesy's classroom. First, Mrs. Creesy arrived. She set her mug of coffee down on her desk and, from her briefcase, took out a notepad that she had scribbled notes on. Then she walked over to the chalkboard. Between sips of coffee and glances at her notepad, Mrs. Creesy made a list on the chalkboard of Oregon Trail topics that she apparently planned to discuss in class that morning. As Mrs. Creesy was doing this, students began to wander into the classroom. Meanwhile, outside the classroom window, Obi saw school buses pulling up in front of the school and letting out students with backpacks on their backs.

It was Liam whom Obi saw first. He entered the

classroom followed by Grace, who was followed by Rachel.

The moment Obi saw Rachel the gerbil knew something was dreadfully wrong. Rachel looked very tired, even a bit haggard, like she hadn't gotten much sleep the night before.

Obi instantly became very concerned. Was Rachel sick? She hadn't come down with a bug, had she? If she had, what was she doing in school, for goodness sake? She should be home, in bed, trying to get better!

The school bell rang as the last few students came rushing into the classroom and plopped down at their desks.

"Good morning, everyone!" Mrs. Creesy said to her students, with a big cheerful smile. She went to her desk and picked up the blue folder. "While we're waiting for Ms. Pearson to make her daily morning announcements, I'm going to hand out your 'My Favorite Pet' papers."

Mrs. Creesy began walking about the classroom, handing each student her or his paper. "You all did very well on this assignment, but *one* of you did exceptionally well. She got an A plus!" said Mrs. Creesy. "And that student is Cleo!"

Obi had no idea which of Mrs. Creesy's students was Cleo—she had only heard Cleo's voice from within Rachel's backpack. It didn't take the gerbil long, though, to identify Cleo. She was the frizzy-haired girl who looked absolutely shocked to find out she had received the best grade in the class. Obi had never seen anyone look so wide-eyed incredulous. Once Cleo got over her shock, her face beamed with delight.

Obi watched as Mrs. Creesy handed Rachel back her homework paper. Mrs. Creesy wasn't looking at the grades as she handed out the papers so, luckily, she didn't notice what Obi had done to Rachel's grade.

Obi saw Rachel's eyes blink in astonishment when she glimpsed the grade she had gotten. She peered up at Mrs. Creesy, with a startled look on her face, but the teacher, busy returning papers, had moved on. A look of confusion came into Rachel's face, like she didn't know quite what to do.

Liam, whose desk was next to Rachel's, happened to glance over at Rachel's paper. He saw the grade on her paper. His mouth dropped open. He got very excited and said something to Rachel. Then he said something to Grace, whose desk was across from his and Rachel's desks. He gestured to the grade on Rachel's paper.

By now, Mrs. Creesy, who was across the classroom, had noticed all the commotion that Liam was causing. She asked, "Is something the matter, Liam?"

"Um, well . . . yeah, actually, there is!"

"And what might that be?"

"Well, Mrs. Creesy, you said Cleo got the best grade. That she got an A plus."

"Yes, that's true," said Mrs. Creesy.

"Well, you gave Rachel an A plus plus!"

Every student in the class looked up when they heard this. Mrs. Creesy frowned. "Excuse me?"

"You gave her an A plus plus! See for yourself!"

Mrs. Creesy came over to where Rachel, Liam, and Grace sat. The other students were all staring in fascination at Rachel, like she was some sort of wierd alien from outer space. Apparently, receiving an A++ from Mrs. Creesy was a highly unusual event. For her part, Cleo, looking extremely concerned, had gotten up from her desk to try and get a peek at the grade on Rachel's paper. She was really craning her neck trying to see.

Mrs. Creesy took the paper from Rachel. She was quiet for a moment as she studied the grade. From her hiding spot in the Oregon Trail covered wagon, Obi could feel her heart thumping wildly inside her chest. She hadn't counted on this. It never occurred to her that Mrs. Creesy would find out about the A plus plus. Obi just assumed Rachel would be the only one to see what Obi had done. What would Mrs. Creesy do when she found out that someone had doctored Rachel's grade? Would she become furious? Would she glance suspiciously around at her students and demand to know who had changed Rachel's grade?

"Hmm," Mrs. Creesy said at last, handing the paper back to Rachel. "My apologies, Rachel. It seems I did give you an A plus plus. It was so late last night when I corrected the last papers, I guess I don't remember having done that. Well, no matter. It was an excellent paper! Well deserving of its A plus plus! I must say, you wrote very compassionately about your pet gerbil, Obi!"

"Thank you," said Rachel. She smiled but, frankly, it wasn't much of a smile. Not for someone who had just gotten an A++! It was a very halfhearted smile, to put it mildly!

Mrs. Creesy noticed how unhappy Rachel looked for she said, "Are you okay, dear?"

"Yeah, I'm okay," replied Rachel in a weepy voice that definitely did not sound like she was okay.

Grace spoke up then. "She's upset because she can't find Obi! He disappeared from his cage!"

Obi was stunned. *She* was the reason Rachel looked so forlorn!?

"Oh, Rachel, I'm so sorry to hear that!" exclaimed Mrs. Creesy, looking very sympathetic.

"He wasn't in his cage yesterday when I got home from school," said Rachel, her voice trembling.

"Well, I do hope he turns up soon," said Mrs. Creesy as she placed a comforting hand on Rachel's shoulder.

Over in the Oregon Trail covered wagon, Obi felt absolutely horrible. She felt so guilty that she had made Rachel feel so sad. It was all Obi could do to keep from leaping out of the covered wagon and racing over and jumping onto Rachel's lap. But Obi didn't dare do such a thing. She knew it would only cause big trouble. Besides, what would Liam do if he saw Obi scurrying toward him on her way to Rachel? The boy was so convinced Obi was a rat, he'd probably faint from fear.

No, as difficult as it would be, Obi would just have to continue to hide out in Mrs. Creesy's classroom until the end of the school day, when she would be able to sneak back into Rachel's backpack and go home with Rachel. The moment Obi was back in the Armstrongs' home, though, nothing—nothing whatsoever—would stop her from magically popping back up in her cage!

Over the school PA system, a woman's loud voice abruptly boomed out: "Good morning, students! This is Ms. Pearson! Time for the Principal's Morning Announcements! I'd like to begin by wishing a very happy birthday to all those whose birthdays it is today! And those students are: Nooowa Zeeerity, Flakey Barfff, Reeeyan Beanteeen, Yooovvvne Wishhhingtooon, and Fattty Muuung!"

It was Mrs. Creesy, of all people, who started to laugh first. She heard the crazy names that Ms.

Pearson had read out over the PA system, and burst into laughter. Then all the students, after first looking quite surprised, began laughing and giggling. Even Rachel, Obi noticed, smiled. A real smile, too!

"Oh, dear!" Ms. Pearson's frantic voice said over the intercom system. "Oh, dear! Oh, dear!" She sounded very flustered. "How did these students' names get all jumbled up and misspelled on my computer!?" she asked, apparently talking to someone else in the principal's office. Evidently, Ms. Pearson was so rattled at having messed up the students' names, she didn't realize she was still talking over the PA system—that everyone in the entire school could hear every word she was saying.

"Where's my stress ball? It's not on my desk where I left it! Has anyone seen my stress ball? I need my stress ball!"

Ms. Pearson became very quiet then. It sounded like someone was whispering to her.

"What!?" Ms. Pearson blurted out. "Oh, my God!"

Then, trying to sound like an unflappable principal again, Ms. Pearson said in a calm voice: "The students I meant to wish happy birthday to are Noah Garrity,

Katey Barth, Ryan Bernstein, Yvonne Washington, and Patty Mung. This ends my morning announcements! Have a good day and happy learning!"

And with that, without even leading the students in the Pledge of Allegiance, Ms. Pearson ended her daily Principal's Morning Announcements, and the PA system was turned off.

From her hiding spot inside the covered wagon, Obi stared at Mrs. Creesy and her students. None of them could stop laughing. Obi knew it was all because of her that Ms. Pearson, the principal, had mangled the names of the students whose birthdays it was that day. And it was all because of her, too, that Ms. Pearson was unable to find her stress ball.

Obi felt bad that she had caused the principal so much distress. But then Obi noticed that Rachel no longer looked so forlorn. In fact, the girl had a *big* grin on her face! Obi had cheered up Rachel. Well, indirectly! How could you feel badly about *that*? You couldn't! At least Obi sure couldn't! Indeed, Obi actually now felt *glad* about what she had done.

Obi's only regret was that she wasn't with Sadie, Coach, Ramona, Pablo, Einstein, and Clarence right at that moment so they could all have a good laugh together at what had just happened.

It took Mrs. Creesy a few moments to regain her composure. It took her even longer to restore quiet in her classroom. Once she had her students' undivided attention again, Mrs. Creesy said, "Well, this certainly has started off to be a most unusual morning!"

Mrs. Creesy walked over to her desk to begin the class lesson.

And that was when *the* most unusual thing of all happened!

To Obi's shock, Mrs. Creesy let out a loud, enormous fart when she sat down at her desk!

It wasn't just Obi who was shocked. Everyone in the classroom looked stunned that Mrs. Creesy would make such a unladylike noise. Mrs. Creesy looked the most startled of all. For a moment, you could've heard a pencil drop on the floor, it was so quiet—but only for a moment. Then someone snorted. Then, all at once, everyone in the classroom burst out laughing—even Mrs. Creesy cracked up!

"Okay, who's the wise guy who put this on my chair?" she asked as she reached under her bum-bum and pulled out a deflated whoopee cushion. That caused everyone to laugh even harder. "Never mind," said Mrs. Creesy, smiling. "Anyway, the shenanigans are over. Time for us to get busy."

And then, turning serious, Mrs. Creesy opened the textbook that was on her desk and said, "Now who remembers where we left off on the Oregon Trail?"

As Mrs. Creesy and her students began discussing the Oregon Trail, Obi couldn't stop thinking about the whoopee cushion. Oh, *she* knew who had put it on Mrs. Creesy's chair. Wouldn't everyone be shocked, she thought, to find it had been a frog! Yes, it was Einstein! Obi remembered how Einstein had mysteriously vanished last night for a short time. None of the other animals knew where he had disappeared to, and Einstein wasn't exactly the most forthcoming frog when he had suddenly reappeared. Well, Obi now knew where and why he had gone off. It was to plant the whoopee cushion on Mrs. Creesy's desk chair.

That Einstein! thought Obi as, smiling to herself, she shook her head in amusement.

Chapter Nineteen

Back to Normal—
Well, Sort of

The rest of that school day went pretty much like any other school day. Which is to say it was pretty uneventful. Which was just how Obi wanted it. She didn't want to stir up any more trouble than she had already caused. She didn't want to do anything that might jeopardize her from being able to sneak back into Rachel's backpack so she could go home with Rachel at the end of the school day. Although she had really enjoyed hanging out with Sadie, Coach, Ramona, Pablo, Einstein, and Clarence and, frankly, would love to have hung out with them that night, too, she also did not want to spend another night away from Rachel. She didn't want to worry her adoptive mother any more than she already had.

So Obi played it safe. She stayed put right there

in that Oregon Trail covered wagon. She kept out of sight—and out of trouble.

When lunchtime came, all the students got up from their desks and, like the day before, left the classroom to go eat lunch in the cafeteria. And like the day before, Mrs. Creesy also left at lunchtime to go to the teachers' lounge, leaving Obi all by herself in the classroom. But *unlike* the day before, Obi did not venture out of the classroom. The moment she was alone, Obi sprang out of the covered wagon, leaped down from the window ledge, dashed across the linoleum-tiled floor to Rachel's cubby, scrambled into the cubby, and hid behind Rachel's backpack. That was where Obi intended to spend the rest of the school day afternoon. She wasn't taking any chances. Not today! She wanted to be able to slip into Rachel's backpack at a moment's notice. Nothing was going to prevent *her* from going back home!

When lunchtime ended, Mrs. Creesy returned to the classroom. A few minutes later, her students poured into the classroom, talking and laughing, and took their seats. Mrs. Creesy waited until the stu-

dents had all settled down before she began that afternoon's lesson. Today's science lesson was on plate
tectonics—the theory that the earth is made up of
huge plates that shift about, causing earthquakes
and volcanic eruptions. At one point, wishing to show
her students which continents formed the plates, Mrs.
Creesy pulled down a wall map of the earth that
hung above the classroom chalkboard. Curious to see
for herself, Obi was about to peek out from behind the
backpack when she noticed that one of Rachel's key
chains that dangled above her head was of the earth.
It had little green continents and blue oceans. Obi
was surprised that she hadn't noticed the key chain
until now. There certainly were a lot of little worlds
in this world! You just had to look for them!

At three o'clock, the last bell of the
day rang. The moment Obi heard
the bell, she knew exactly what to
do. She slipped into the outside
pocket of Rachel's backpack.
The moment Mrs. Creesy's
students heard the bell,
they, too, knew exactly

what to do. They leaped up from desks, went to their cubbies, and grabbed their backpacks. Concealed in the outer pocket of Rachel's backpack, Obi felt her stomach lurch a little as Rachel swung her backpack up over her shoulder. Then off went Rachel—and off went Obi—out of the classroom, through the hallway, out the main entrance of the school, across the school plaza, and into one of the waiting, idling school buses.

As Obi rode home on the bus inside Rachel's backpack (which Rachel held on her lap while she sat with Grace), the little gerbil wondered how, once finally home, she was going to sneak out of the backpack and slip back into her cage without being spotted by Rachel. Obi was really stressing out about it. As things turned out, though, she had no need to worry. The moment Rachel walked in through the front door of her house, she dropped her backpack on the floor of the front hallway and eagerly rushed off to go tell her mother about the A++ she had received on her homework paper.

Obi waited until Rachel's excited footsteps faded. Then, moving quickly, the little gerbil pulled herself up out of the outside pocket of the backpack and hopped

down onto the slate floor. Obi paused to see where she was, to get her bearings. She was near the grandfather clock that stood by the carpeted stairs that led up to the Armstrongs' bedrooms.

Suddenly, who should step out of the kitchen and into the front hallway, but Kenobi! The golden retriever puppy spotted Obi and came right over.

"*OBI!*" he cried happily, his tail swishing back and forth.

"Hawo, Kenobi!" replied Obi.

"What are you doing downstairs?" Kenobi asked. "You know Mom has been looking all over for you!"

"She has?"

"Yes, she has! Hey, want to throw me a ball?" asked Kenobi, his eyes glistening with excitement. "Throw me a ball! Throw me a ball!"

"Sorry, Kenobi, but I can't!" said Obi. "I'm in a big rush! I need to get back to my cage!"

Obi gave the dog a little wave and disappeared behind the grandfather clock. She entered the little mouse hole that was in the wall down by the floor—it was the front hallway entrance to the secret passageway.

Obi was hurrying through the secret passageway toward Rachel's bedroom when, up ahead, she spied a tiny, dark figure, lurking in the shadowy light. As dark as it was, Obi knew who *this* creature was.

"Well, hawo, Mr. Durkins!"

The old mouse looked startled to see Obi. "Kid, you're back!"

"Yes, I'm back!" replied Obi. "And I've got news for you, Mr. Durkins! You know that homework paper Rachel had to write? The one about her favorite pet? The one you made me think couldn't possibly be about me? Well, guess what? It *was* about me!"

No sooner had Obi said this when she realized

something. "But you knew that, didn't you, Mr. Durkins? Since you know everything that happens in this house, you knew she wrote about me, didn't you?"

Obi expected Mr. Durkins to deny that he could possibly know such a thing, but he didn't. "Yeah, I knew," he said.

"Then why did you make me think she didn't write about me?"

But once again, when she heard herself ask this, Obi knew the answer. "You were just being your usual, evil Mr. Durkins self, weren't you?"

"You're a rodent, kid! A furry, little rodent with whiskers and a tail! It's not healthy for you to be loved by a human! You've got no business being a human's favorite pet!"

As angry as Obi was at Mr. Durkins, she couldn't help but feel a little sorry for the disgruntled, old mouse. He was so filled with hate and bitterness, he would never be anyone's favorite *anything*!

"I hope some day, Mr. Durkins, you'll understand the meaning of love," said Obi.

"Love!" scoffed Mr. Durkins. "Like you know what *love* is!"

"But I do know!"

"All I can say is, I sure am glad I have Wan I can count on!" declared Mr. Durkins. "At least *he* knows he's a rodent!"

"Oh, I know I'm a rodent, Mr. Durkins," said Obi. "But I also know what it's like to be loved and how nice it is to be someone's favorite pet!"

Obi was about to tell Mr. Durkins that she planned to undo every evil thing that he had taught Wan, but then she realized she didn't have time for that.

"Excuse me, Mr. Durkins, but I have a cage to get back to!"

Obi squeezed past the old, crippled mouse and hurried on her way. Obi got to the tiny hole that led out into Rachel's bedroom. She was so anxious to return to her cage, she stepped out into Rachel's bedroom without even looking to see if Rachel or one of the three cats was in the room. Luckily, none of them were. Only Wan was.

Obi raced across the bedroom floor to the side of Rachel's dresser. With her two front paws, she grabbed hold of the lamp cord that dangled down from the side of the dresser. She climbed up the cord in a matter of seconds. As Obi scurried past Wan's cage to get to her own cage, she called out, "Hawo, Wan!"

Wan was in the bottom part of his cage, crawling about in the deep drifts of cedar shavings that lined the floor. He poked his head up out of the pile of cedar shavings and peered quizzically about.

"*Obi!?*" he said. He looked startled. "Where have you been? What are you doing out of your cage?"

But Obi was in too much of a rush to stop and chat with Wan. She dashed to the front of her cage, rose up onto her hind legs, pushed open the little square door with her two front paws, and scrambled into her cage. With the end of her tail, she snapped the cage door shut behind her.

Now that she was safely back in her home, Obi turned to Wan and said, "By the way, Wan, you and I need to talk! You have some serious behavioral issues that we need to work on! But don't worry, Wan, I'll help you overcome them!"

As Obi was saying this, Rachel walked into her bedroom. Her gaze instantly fell upon Obi inside her cage. The girl froze. She stared at Obi with the most incredulous eyes.

"Obi!?" she exclaimed. Then, becoming very excited, she cried out, "You're back!"

Rachel rushed over to her dresser and took Obi out of her cage. She looked absolutely delighted to see Obi again. She couldn't stop smiling as she held Obi in the palm of one hand and stroked Obi's little head with the tip of her index finger of her other hand. "Oh, I'm so glad to see you!" she said.

But then Rachel's face darkened, and her eyes narrowed. "Where have you been, Mister?" she demanded.

Obi gave her adoptive mother a very bewildered look, like she had no idea what Rachel could possibly be talking about.

"You're able to escape from your cage, aren't you?"

Obi tried to look even more befuddled. *Escape from my cage!? Me!!? What are you talking about, Mom!?*

"You know what *I* think?" Rachel said. "*I* think there's something you're not telling me, Obi!"

Oh, there sure was! Actually, there were quite a number of things! But, seriously, how could Obi ever tell Rachel all the things she would love to tell her when Obi only spoke Gerbil and Rachel only spoke Human?

"Well," said Rachel. "As far as you escaping from your cage goes, I suppose that—"

Rachel abruptly stopped what she was saying. The reason she stopped was because of Wan. That infuriating little gerbil had begun to gnaw on the front bars of his cage, distracting Rachel.

Obi desperately wanted to hear what Rachel had been about to say! "Finish what you were about to say, Mom!" Obi squeaked, speaking in Gerbil. "What about me escaping from my cage? What do you suppose?"

Rachel let out a weary groan. "There he goes again!" she said, flashing an exasperated look at Wan. "Do you *have* to do that, Wan?" Then, to Obi, she said, "I don't know how you do it, Obi! I really don't! That gnawing drives me up a wall! But you're so kind and patient and understanding, you never get mad at Wan, do you?"

If Obi knew how to speak Human, she would've said, "Trust me, Mom, I'm not all *that* kind and patient and understanding!" She also would've told Rachel not to worry, that she, Obi, was going to unteach every evil thing Mr. Durkins had ever taught Wan—including that nasty habit he had of gnawing on the bars of his cage!

Rachel began to put Obi back into her cage when she suddenly stopped.

"Oh!" Rachel cried out excitedly. "I know what I haven't told you, Obi! Guess what happened in school today? I got an A plus plus on my homework paper! You'll never guess who I wrote about!"

With the most innocent, most curious, most angelic look on her whiskered gerbil face, Obi peered up into Rachel's happy, glistening eyes.

"I wrote about *you*, Obi! Yes, *you*! My teacher, Mrs. Creesy, gave me an A plus plus! She's never given anyone an A plus plus before! *Never!* Not even to Cleo!

And *she's* the smartest kid in the class! You must be a good-luck gerbil, Obi, that's all I can say!"

And with that, Rachel put Obi back into her cage and left the room, probably, no doubt, to go tell others about the big news, that she had gotten an amazing A++ from Mrs. Creesy.

If only she knew.

Obi never forgot her friends at school. In the days and weeks that followed, Obi often thought about Sadie, Coach, Ramona, Pablo, Einstein, and Clarence, and wondered what they were up to. She missed them, she missed them a lot. Even months later, she still chuckled at the things they all did together that night she was with them.

It wasn't just her school friends, though, that Obi missed—she missed their whole world. It was a world Obi would love to be a part of. But of course, that could never happen. How could it? Obi lived in the Armstrongs' home; they lived at school! Unless there was a sudden shift in the earth's plate tectonics, causing Rachel's school to collide and become part of Rachel's home, it was highly unlikely the two worlds could ever be one world—as nice of a thought as that was!

Late one evening not long after Obi's overnight school adventure, when the lights in Rachel's bedroom were off and Rachel was in her bunk bed, sound asleep, and Wan was in his cage, sound asleep, Obi was in her cage, thinking about her friends at school. Suddenly, she thought of something. She never did find out how her school friends escaped from their cages! She kept meaning to ask them that night, but, somehow, she had totally forgotten! Now, regrettably, she would never be able to ask them!

Obi sighed. It was a deep, wistful sigh. There were so many things Obi would like to ask Sadie, Coach, Ramona, Pablo, Einstein, and Clarence. What were their favorite things to do in school? Is it really a big surprise when a teacher pulls a surprise quiz? What do you do on school holidays when school is closed?

Obi told herself that if she ever got to see her school friends again, she would definitely have to remember to ask them these things. But then again, maybe she wouldn't. Maybe like that night she was at school, she would get so caught up in the moment, having so much fun, she'd forget to ask, only to remember it later when things went back to normal—well, sort of normal. Things could never, of course, go back to normal completely. They couldn't! That's what happens when you have a really good friend. Or friends. They change you, just as you change them, in ways you never thought possible.

All of sudden, Obi could have sworn she heard something over in Rachel's bedroom closet. It sounded like a little creature padding about. Was it Mr. Durkins? If it was him, what was he doing snooping about in Rachel's closet? In the darkness, Obi peered at the closet door. She had to really strain her eyes to be able to  see, it was so dark in the room. The closet door was slightly ajar. As Obi gazed at the door, it dawned on her that she had never been in Rachel's bedroom closet before! Not once! Well, she'd just have to change that, wouldn't she? It would be an adventure, she thought, investigating Rachel's bedroom closet. A new world!

Like going off to school!